# HILARY McKAY

# PUDDING BAG SCHOOL

## The Birthday Wish

Hodder
Children's
Books

A division of Hachette Children's Books

## CHAPTER ONE

Simon Percy was ten years old on the last day
of the summer holidays. That year, instead of
a birthday party, he had a picnic in the park.

"Then you can ask a crowd," said Gran.

Simon was not at all sure that he wanted a
crowd. He thought there could not be a more
unlucky day of the year to have a birthday.
He knew that the people invited would be
sure to talk about school, and he did not think
he could bear it.

That was why the birthday picnic ended up
having only two guests, Dougal McDougal

and Madeline Brown. Simon was almost certain he could trust Dougal and Madeline not to ruin his birthday, but just to make sure he added an extra line to the top of their invitations.

## PLEASE ONLY COME IF YOU PROMISE NOT TO TALK ABOUT TOMORROW

The picnic was spread out under an enormous beech tree. It was a feast of salads and sausages and surprises and strawberries. By the time Simon and Dougal and Madeline had finished the strawberries they were stretched out flat in the leafy shade, too full to bend in the middle.

All afternoon the forbidden subject had not been mentioned.

It was Simon himself who said the word.

"School in the morning," said Simon.

Madeline and Dougal remembered the

instructions in their invitations and did not reply, but Gran reached out a comforting hand.

"Surely not!" she murmured, rubbing her great-grandson's hair as she spoke, and noticing at the same time how much it looked and felt like the trodden, end-of-summer grass of the park. "Surely not! You worry too much Simon! Come now, it is time for the cake!"

Madeline, Dougal and Simon rolled over to watch the solemn lighting of the candles. In the bright September sunshine the flames were almost invisible.

"Ten!" said Gran. "Enough to go all the way round the cake! Now then, Dougal and Madeline!" And she led the singing of Happy Birthday.

"Thank you," said Simon, when the song and the three cheers that followed had ended.

"It wasn't very loud," said Dougal. "Even

with me. Three is not really enough to sing properly. Never mind though. Most people have more family than Simon! That's the difference!"

"Shut up Dougal McDougal!" said Madeline at once.

"Simon doesn't mind," said Dougal. "Do you Simon?"

"No," said Simon, who actually minded very much indeed.

"Well then," said Dougal robustly. "We can't not talk about everything! And Simon's mum and dad! Very weird! Disappeared, just like that!"

"No, Dougal, they did not disappear, just like that!" corrected Gran. "They went on holiday when Simon was six weeks old."

"Yes, but what a holiday!" exclaimed Dougal.

"A ten day hot-air ballooning holiday," said

Gran. "Or supposed to be!" and she sighed regretfully.

"Are you sure it was days?" asked Madeline.

"Perfectly sure my dear. Why?"

"Because if it was years," explained Madeline, "ten years, not ten days, they'd be back quite soon, wouldn't they?"

"I never thought of that!" exclaimed Simon excitedly, but Gran shook her head.

"I should never have agreed to years," she told Madeline. " 'Ten days,' they said. 'In the foothills of the Himalayas! It is the chance of a lifetime!' 'Well,' I told them, 'In that case you had better go and do not hurry back if you are enjoying yourselves ...' And then nothing but that postcard when Simon was three ... Wish You Were Here!"

"Hadn't Simon better blow his candles out?" asked Dougal suddenly. "They've nearly burnt down to the icing!"

Gran glanced at the cake and saw that Dougal was quite right.

"The sooner the better, Simon!" she urged, but Simon hesitated, saving up the moments that were left. When the candles were gone it would be the end of his birthday tea, the end of summer, and he would be officially ten years old. He sighed, and the sigh mixed up with a puff of wind and the flames blew out. There was a brief scattering of sparks across the chocolate icing and the smallest thread of smoke in the air, and the magic was over.

"Quick Simon!" said Madeline urgently. "Make your birthday wish!"

Thank goodness for Madeline! thought Simon. Her astonishing suggestion was still in his mind, and he knew exactly what his wish should be. He squeezed his eyes tight shut as he made it.

"Done!" he said a minute later, and opened

his eyes just as the first crisp leaf of autumn came tumbling down. It landed on the birthday cake, fiery gold and shaped like a star.

"What did you wish for, then?" asked Dougal, but Simon shook his head and refused to tell.

Gradually the afternoon turned to evening and the park began to empty. Dougal McDougal's seven grown-up sisters arrived in a posse and took him captive. Madeline Brown's genius professor father wandered into the park and across to the beech tree to collect his daughter.

"Thank you Mrs Percy, and thank you Simon," Madeline said as she got up to leave. "I've had a lovely time."

"My wife," said Madeline's father to Simon, "... er ... Mrs Brown ... Madeline's mother ... has asked me to wish you a very happy ...

a very happy ..."

He looked helplessly at Madeline. For a genius, he was a very forgetful man.

"A very happy birthday," said Madeline. "Where is mother today?"

"Parachute jumping," her father told her as he solemnly shook Simon's hand. "Strange but true. It is turning into quite a worrying habit, isn't it Madeline?"

"She just likes the excitement," Simon heard Madeline say soothingly as she led him away, and then she turned to wave a last goodbye, and was gone.

It seemed suddenly lonely under the beech tree without Dougal and Madeline. Simon was glad to help pack up the remains of the picnic and go home. There, while Gran sipped China tea from her special pink cup, he arranged and admired his birthday presents.

He had five.

A large box of chocolates from Dougal.

Invisible ink felt pens given by Madeline.

From Gran a pair of binoculars, a small cockatoo, and a book called *A Practical Guide to Space Exploration*.

Simon opened the chocolates, wrote an invisible ink thank you letter to Gran, polished the binoculars, coaxed the cockatoo out of her cage and tidied *A Practical Guide to Space Exploration* carefully out of sight. Simon had a whole bookshelf of books, all birthday presents and chosen by Gran, who liked to think of him reading something useful. Earlier that day Madeline had read the titles outloud.

"*A Child's Guide to Modern Technology*
*Metal Work for Beginners*
*Junk Modelling that Works*
*Navigation for Nine-Year-Olds*
*Self Help for the Under-Sixes*
*Anybody Can Do Anything* and *How Does It Go?*

*Where the Wild Things Are."*

"What lovely books!" Madeline had exclaimed. "Have you read them all?"

Simon shook his head. He had not read any of them except *Where the Wild Things Are* which Gran had bought by mistake, thinking it was Natural History. He took it to bed with him to read again that night and one of the wild things got into his dreams and turned into a monster.

A monster that Simon knew very well.

Mr Bang Bang Jones.

Mr B B Jones (often known as Old Bang Bang) was the Headmaster of Pudding Bag School, and he was also the reason for the extra line on Simon's party invitations.

Mr B B Jones was what Dougal McDougal described as a second-hand spaceman. Once he had been an astronaut.

The children of Pudding Bag School had

discovered that second-hand astronauts made very bad headmasters, and Mr Bang Bang Jones had made up his mind from the start that Headmastering in no way compared to exploring unknown galaxies. Still, he had hopes of it one day leading to higher things. His books on Headmastering Techniques sold very well, and the children (whom he treated as alien life forms) were quite useful for research purposes if kept properly under control ... Simon turned restlessly in bed. Last term his class teacher had left suddenly and with no explanation (this was not at all unusual in Pudding Bag School) and Mr Bang Bang Jones had taken over the class instead ...

"School tomorrow," moaned Simon in his dreams.

Across the street the church clock chimed three, and Simon, who had been dreaming he arrived at school wearing nothing at all, woke up. Three o'clock, and school in six hours and where was his uniform? He rolled sleepily out of bed and groped through cupboards and drawers until it was finally collected. Then he piled it all on a chair and climbed back into bed.

Then he climbed out of bed again and put it on, all of it, even the jacket.

Finally he lay back down again, his arms and legs arranged in straight lines, like a stick man falling through space, so as not to crease anything. The church clock struck four.

Outside the window a shooting star dropped through the sky.

Simon curled into a sudden tight ball and fell fast asleep.

## CHAPTER TWO

Simon's gran was not very good with time.
She had lived through so much of it. Tens of
thousands of days, hundreds of thousands of
hours. A few minutes here or there meant
nothing to Gran anymore. That was why
she simply could not understand the fuss
Simon was making about eating a little bowl
of cereal.

"You must have breakfast," she told him
patiently. "Breakfast is important!"

"Old Bang Bang Jones thinks being on time
is important," said Simon. "Old Bang Bang's

18

really terrible, Gran!"

"When things were terrible," said Gran slowly, looking far, far past Simon into the tens of thousands of days behind her. "I used to say, 'This will pass.' And it did. It always did. It always does."

Simon abandoned his shredded wheat and got up to give Gran a sudden tight hug. It felt to him as if he had been ten for a very long time.

Once Simon was out of the house all desire to rush to school deserted him. He plodded along Pudding Bag Lane in a muddle of fear. He knew he was late, but all the same he went more and more slowly. There was a small sweet shop outside the school gates and he paused to inspect its shabby window display.

Nothing looked very enticing. There were ancient boxes of penny chews, bubble-gum in faded wrappers, damp flying saucers and melting red bootlaces. The back of the shop, as always, disappeared into darkness. A notice on the door read "OPEN when absolutely necessary". It was, as usual, locked.

A poster in the window caught Simon's attention. It was an advertisement for an agency and it was the only thing that looked new.

*SIMPLY THE BEST SUPPLIES AND SERVICES!*
(it said in curly letters)

*For Household Pets, Professional Staff,*
*Vacuum Cleaner Parts.*
*Dry Cleaning, Spring Cleaning,*
*Caretakers and Cooks.*
*Fine Jewels, Fireworks, First Class Free Advice.*

*Enquire Within!*
*All Needs Supplied!*
*Everything Guaranteed Best In All The World!*

Underneath, in ordinary writing, someone had added, (Cockatoos and Caretakers temporarily out of stock).

Simon read it three times and such was his state of mind that he did not even notice the mention of cockatoos.

Register was over by the time Simon finally arrived at school. The whole class was seated and listening to a new teacher. A new teacher! thought Simon, his heart leaping with relief. And there was Dougal McDougal waving across the room to him. Simon flopped down beside him and sighed with relief and Dougal kindly whispered the new teacher's name.

"Miss Leatherbottom!" whispered Dougal McDougal.

*From the diary of Simon Percy. Tuesday 9th September*

*We have got a new class teacher. NOT MR BANG*

*BANG JONES!!!!*

Simon outlined the words in red and drew stars and rockets round the edge. He could hardly believe his luck. No Mr Jones with his thunderous noise and his fuming, volcanic silences. No Mr Jones, staring and glaring and handing out punishments. No Mr Jones with his cries of, "Simon Percy! Wake up! You might be the original Pudding Bag of Pudding Bag Lane!"

*Our new teacher has given us each a book to be our diaries to fill in whenever we have an empty moment,* wrote Simon that morning. *Dougal McDougal who is my best friend has filled in his for the week already. He says he knows what will happen. Our new teacher is ...*

Simon Percy paused for several moments,

staring into space.

... *magic,* wrote Simon, finding the right word
at last.

"I've been scared all holiday that we would
have Mr Jones for Class teacher again," he
whispered to Dougal.

"Old Bang Bang," said Dougal McDougal
scornfully. "He's nothing but a second-hand
spaceman! I don't know why everyone's so
frightened of Old Bang Bang! I bet she's not!"

Dougal nodded towards the stock cupboard
where the new teacher, invisible except for a
pair of sparkling green shoes, was busy with
an enormous list.

"I bet ..." began Dougal again, and stopped
as suddenly as if he had been switched off.

A sudden noise had shaken the windows.
The whole class froze and the new teacher's

startled face popped hurriedly round the stock cupboard door.

"Whatever was that?" she asked.

"It was Mr Jones' office door," Dougal McDougal told her. "Slamming!"

"It sounded like the roof falling off!"

"And that's him coming down the corridor now. That smacking noise. It's his feet."

"Good Heavens!"

"Everyone's scared of him," continued Dougal, "except me and Madeline Brown."

"Madeline Brown?"

"The one with plaits. He's coming this way."

"Madeline Brown, please open the door," said the new teacher, suddenly taking control. "Then the headmaster need not knock ..."

"He never knocks," said Dougal, helpful to the last. "He just gives a wopping great bash ..."

The wopping great bash came just at that

moment and would have flattened Madeline
Brown completely had not her teacher
swooped across the room and rescued her
just in time.

Mr B B Jones, Old Bang Bang, Second-hand
astronaut and terror of Pudding Bag School,
was in the room.

"Sit down!" he ordered Madeline
pompously. "I do not encourage skulking
behind doors. Ah! The new teacher! Grave
doubts! Grave doubts!"

"I beg your pardon?" said the new teacher.

"Still, you are only here temporarily,
depending upon satisfaction ..."

"I am sure I shall be satisfied," said the new
teacher not very calmly. "Madeline dear, go
and sit down since you are not hurt."

"My satisfaction!" interrupted Mr Bang Bang
Jones, who was clearly on the point of
explosion. "And I will warn you in advance

that Class 4b, Pudding Bag School, Pudding Bag Lane, is by far the worst in the school as regards application, concentration, multiplication, subtraction, coherent explanation and remembering to bring back notes from home. In fact, it was because of their exceptionally primitive behaviour that I made use of them for my research last term."

"I am very much looking forward to working with them!"

"Alien life forms in all but habitation," continued Mr Bang Bang Jones, pinky purple with crossness at being interrupted, "I shall need them again so do not spoil them, Miss er ... Miss er ... Young Miss! Hard work and silence! Also Science, Mathematics, form filling, and periods of extreme boredom to prepare them for future life. But science is the thing! I should like to see them all exploring Outer Space!"

"They are far too young," said the new teacher unhelpfully, and clearly not at all pleased at being addressed as Young Miss.

"Now Mr Jones, I have been going through the stock cupboard and making a list of our most urgent requirements. I find we need poster paints, coloured paper, scissors, glue, glitter, paintbrushes, gold and silver ink (for marking), a new sweet tin, a new biscuit tin, story books (at least two hundred), several computers, a piano, Christmas decorations, and comics and games for wet playtimes."

"What? What!" shouted Mr Bang Bang Jones.

"Poster paints, coloured paper, scissors, glue, glitter, new brushes, gold and silver ink (for marking), a new sweet tin, a new biscuit tin, story books (at least two hundred), several computers, a piano, Christmas decorations, comics and games for wet playtimes, and games equipment."

"Games equipment?"

"Footballs, netballs, tennis balls, basket balls, rounders bats, hoops, mats, ropes and a trampolene. Skittles, sacks, eggs and spoons ..."

Mr Jones, who had been staring at her with a mixture of fury and astonishment on his face, suddenly smiled.

"Most amusing," he said. "Most amusing," and without another word he stalked out of the room.

Class 4b sighed with relief.

"What a lot of huffing and puffing!" said the new teacher cheerfully.

"I told you she wouldn't be scared of him," whispered Dougal McDougal.

*Miss Leatherbottom is very pretty. Her hair is the colour of the leaf that fell on my birthday cake and her dress is shining green.*

*Your diaries are private matters, she said to us all. So I shall resist reading them. But Simon why do you keep asking me how to spell leather bottom?*

*Because I am writing about you, I said.*

*Oh, she said, but I have not got ... why do you think? ... WHAT are you putting Simon Percy?*

*And then she read this diary although she had just said they should be private. And then she said Copy This Down and wrote on the blackboard.*

*My class teacher's name is Miss Gilhoolie NOT MISS LEATHERBOTTOM.*


Gran's little house was one of those which backed on to the playing fields of Pudding Bag School. At morning break Simon ran out into the playground, looked up at his bedroom window and there was the cockatoo, looking back down at him.

"Oh Miss LeatherGilhoolie!" cried Simon,

rushing back into the classroom in great excitement. "Come and see my cockatoo!"

Too late he saw that she was not alone.

"Your teacher does not wish to see your cockatoo!" snapped the furious voice of Mr Bang Bang Jones.

"Of course I wish to see Simon's cockatoo," exclaimed Miss Gilhoolie immediately.

"Your teacher is about to make a very important purchase on behalf of you all," continued Mr Jones, ignoring her completely. "A signed edition (in three volumes) at a mere forty-nine pounds ninety-five pence per volume of my own privately published work," and he waved his hand to indicate three enormous black books arranged on Miss Gilhoolie's desk.

PRACTICAL PUNISHMENTS

ALL FULLY TRIED AND TESTED

31

WITH COLOUR ILLUSTRATIONS

BY

B.B. JONES (SIR)

"They sound absolutely dreadful!" said Miss
Gilhoolie.

"Thank you, thank you!" said Mr Bang Bang
Jones, rubbing his hands together in delight.
"They are absolutely dreadful. That is the
whole point. And how many sets would you
like to purchase? One for home and one to
keep in the classroom of course. And some for
Christmas presents perhaps? All profits to a
private very good cause."

"What very good cause?" asked Miss
Gilhoolie suspiciously.

"A private very good cause," repeated Mr
Jones peevishly, not wishing to explain his
secret hope of saving enough money to bribe

NASA to let him back into their rockets. "Shall we say three copies, Miss Gilhoolie? Nine volumes?"

"I think not, Mr Jones," said Miss Gilhoolie, very politely. "And now please excuse me. I have been invited to see a cockatoo."

Mr Bang Bang Jones looked shocked. "Kindly explain yourself!" he said.

"I shall not be buying any of your books," explained Miss Gilhoolie, very kindly indeed.

"But no one has ever refused before!"

"It is a great shame that I should be the first."

"Impertinent and unprofessional!"

"Mr Jones!" said Miss Gilhoolie reprovingly. "Come Simon!"

"You will regret this Young Miss!" roared the headmaster at her departing back, but Miss Gilhoolie simply shrugged a sparkling shoulder and waved a cheerful hand.

"Miss Leatherbo ..." began Simon when they

were halfway across the playground. "I mean Miss Gilhooliebottom ... I mean Miss LeatherGilhoolie?"

"Yes Simon?"

"Hadn't you better buy those books? The other teachers do."

"No Simon."

"It would please Mr Jones. Then he might not be so cross."

"I expect there are other ways of pleasing Mr Jones," said Miss Gilhoolie. "What does he like, besides selling books?"

"Space," said Simon. He's a second-hand spaceman, didn't you know? He really went there once, in a rocket. But they would never let him go again because he quarrelled so much with the other astronauts."

"Who told you that?" asked Miss Gilhoolie laughing. "Dougal McDougal?"

"No. Everyone knows. It's really true!"

"Poor Mr Jones!"

"Poor Mr Jones!" exclaimed Dougal McDougal, overhearing as Simon and the new teacher came into the playing field. "Poor Mr Jones! I thought you were on our side!"

"I am not on any side," said Miss Gilhoolie with dignity. "I am simply here to do my best! Now then Simon, where is this wonderful birthday present?"

Simon forgot Mr Bang Bang Jones, and concentrated instead on pointing out the perfections of his cockatoo, clearly visible as a small white dot.

"It was clever of your gran to get you binoculars too," Madeline Brown commented.

"Was it?"

"Of course. With them you can see her easily from the playground."

"See Gran?"

"See your cockatoo!"

"Oh," said Simon, wishing he had thought of that.

"Madeline Brown is very brainy," he remarked to Dougal that lunchtime.

"Not compared to me she isn't."

"Compared to me she is!"

"Oh well," began Dougal McDougal cheerfully, "compared to you ... Oh, never mind!"

"Never mind what?"

"Nothing," said Dougal, changing the subject. "I tell you what, Old Bang Bang doesn't think much of Miss Gilhoolie, does he?"

"No," agreed Simon. "And she won't buy his books. I heard her telling him so."

"Is she brave?" wondered Dougal McDougal, "or is she daft? Brave or daft, Simon?"

"Brave," said Simon.

*Simon Percy's diary. Wednesday, 10th September*

*We were talking about hobbies this morning. Madeline Brown told Miss Gilhoolie that hers was theoretical parachute jumping, and Dougal McDougal said his was getting away from his sisters, and Miss Gilhoolie said, And what about you Simon?*

*And I said would you mind if I called my cockatoo after you Miss Gilhoolie only have you got another name because I don't think Leatherbottom sounds right for a cockatoo.*

*What about Featherbottom then? asked Dougal McDougal, nearly dead with laughing but Miss Gilhoolie said, Thank you Simon, you are very kind and my other name is Guinevere.*

*But she couldn't stop laughing at Dougal.*

*Guinevere my cockatoo.*

*We have got a caretaker now at Pudding Bag*

School. Dougal McDougal says we must have had one before but nobody ever saw him. But everyone sees Mr Bedwig. He works very hard. Already he has caught Dougal McDougal eating his dinner on the bike shed roof and mended the radiators and polished the doorknobs and got up all the chewing gum that was stuck to the playground.

"And any more that I find will go to the police for genetic fingerprinting," Mr Bedwig had announced when the last piece was removed, "and whoever spat it out will get What For From Me! And you can get down from that roof Bonnie Prince Charlie. I'm having none of that."

"How did you know I was up here?" asked Dougal, sensibly realising that he had met his match at last, and scrambling down.

"Look at you, all over green muck!" scolded Mr Bedwig, handing him a duster to dust himself down. "How did I know you were up there? I have been a caretaker since the year dot, and I know your sort with that red hair. My family were caretakers in the ark. Between us we have Seen It All."

Dougal stared.

"And who is your friend over there?" asked Mr Bedwig. "Talking to the little girl with plaits."

"Oh him!" said Dougal McDougal. "He is Simon Percy but we call him Simple Simon. He is very quiet."

"Percy is a good old name and he doesn't look simple to me," said Mr Bedwig, "and quiet, in my experience, means brains."

"Brains!" said Dougal to Simon, as if it was a great joke. "I wonder if Miss Leatherbottom thinks the same!"

Dougal was always doing that, calling Miss Gilhoolie Miss Leatherbottom in private.

It muddled Simon terribly. He mixed up the names all the time.

"Really Simon!" snapped Miss Gilhoolie at last.

Simon hung his head.

"Simon!" hissed Dougal, poking him. "Don't just sit there! Say sorry to Miss Leatherbottom!"

"Sorry Miss Leatherbottom," said Simon, and the whole class collapsed.

This upset Simon so much that at break he went out into the playground and picked a fight with Dougal McDougal.

## CHAPTER THREE

The fight between Simon Percy and Dougal McDougal had hardly started when Mr Bedwig emerged suddenly from the boiler house and plucked them apart.

"I have never seen the like!" he exclaimed. "Dougal McDougal, you should be ashamed! Look at the state of him, and not a mark on you!"

"But he ..."

"Not a word!" interrupted Mr Bedwig, cutting off Dougal's protests at once. "Into school with you please, and no argy-bargy!

Simon Percy, go straight to the cloakroom
and brush yourself down. There is half the
playground stuck on the back of that jumper
of yours! Now hop it!"

Simon hopped it without a word, but
Dougal McDougal, outraged at being blamed
for a fight he had not begun, had to be
escorted from the battlefield and delivered
(still protesting) to a most unsympathetic
Miss Gilhoolie.

"Fighting!" she exclaimed crossly. "I thought
you and Simon were friends, Dougal! Poor
Simon!"

She also refused to listen to any kind of
argy-bargy.

In the cloakroom Simon wiped his nose,
brushed down his clothes, and washed away
the dirt and tears that Mr Bedwig had so
kindly pretended not to see. Then he opened
the lost property cupboard and crawled inside

and was discovered almost at once by
Mr Bedwig.

"Out of that young Simon!" he ordered
firmly. "Before you catch something nasty.
There's places in this school worse than the
ark on the thirty-ninth day! I wasn't sent a
moment too soon!"

"Were you sent?" asked Simon, as he
crawled obediently out. "Who by?"

"Agency," said Mr Bedwig, tutting with
disgust as he turned over a pile of mouldering
plimsolls. "Now you should be back in the
classroom, young man! That red-headed friend
of yours is there already and has caught it hot
and strong from your Miss Gilhoolie!"

"Has he?"

"She is a proper cracker, your new teacher,"
continued Mr Bedwig. "Just what we need!
I shall get her desk stopped wobbling tonight.
It is dropping to bits and her blackboard could

do with a coat of paint. Now then, quick march! She is worrying about you!"

There was no use protesting. Before he knew it Simon was back in the classroom. There he had to stand up while Dougal said, "Sorry I bumped you over but you pushed me first so I don't see why I am getting all the blame!"

"That's quite enough!" interrupted Miss Gilhoolie. "Sit down please and I will read a story to cheer us all up."

"You started it!" whispered Simon to Dougal as soon as Miss Gilhoolie was well under way.

"I'm not sorry," Dougal hissed back. "I said I was, but I'm not. And I think you ought to say sorry for making me say sorry!"

"You and your Leatherbottoms!" said Simon.

Miss Gilhoolie paused in her reading.

"It was a trick! It was meant to be funny," muttered Dougal.

"She HATES being called Miss Leatherbottom!" replied Simon, and then Miss Gilhoolie banged her book shut and said she was not reading to such rude, ungrateful people any longer.

"You can write up your diaries until the bell goes!" she ordered. "And no wailing! Or it will be worse. It will be table tests!"

The quarrel between Simon and Dougal lasted all Friday morning and right through lunch. Simon was so upset that he had not even the heart to go out and wave to Guinevere. Instead he took refuge in the cloakroom again, and once again was discovered by Mr Bedwig.

"I don't know what you are thinking of!" exclaimed Mr Bedwig. "There's never been a battle won yet from under a heap of coats! You are letting down the family name and no mistake! The Percys in the past never hid! Knights in armour since the court of King Arthur, the Percys have been."

"Oh," said Simon, and then, remembering something. "You know you said you were sent from an agency, Mr Bedwig? Was it the one that the notice in the sweet shop is about? Everything guaranteed best in all the world?"

"And why not?"

"I wonder if that's where Gran got my

cockatoo from."

"If I were you I would get out into the sunshine young Percy, and stop wondering quite so much."

"What was the ark like on the thirty-ninth day?"

"According to my dad it was far from sparkling," said Mr Bedwig, shepherding Simon towards the door. "Far from! Damp was not the word for it! And no pumps either! It was bail or to the bottom! And you think you have problems! Out you go and give that cockatoo a wave before the bell goes!"

Simon went, and on the doorstep almost fell over Madeline Brown who was sitting with her chin on her knees and an expression of great concentration on her face.

"It would be terrible if old Bang Bang got rid of Miss Gilhoolie," she said.

"How could he?" asked Simon.

"He's been staring out of his window all this time," said Madeline, ignoring Simon's question. "She's been out here teaching Dougal the Highland Fling and he's been watching with a face like ... a face like ... well, even worse than it usually is, and I suddenly thought ..."

"What?"

"How terrible it would be if he got rid of Miss Gilhoolie," said Madeline.

The Highland Fling must have had a good effect on Dougal McDougal. At the end of afternoon school he dashed back into the classroom where Simon, last as usual, was getting ready to go home, and pushed a note into his hand before charging back outside again.

ALL RIGHT. PEACE. PAX. FRIENDS.

"Peace Pax Friends!" read Simon aloud, and then, needing to tell someone the good news, ran off down the corridors to find Mr Bedwig.

"Mr Bedwig! Mr Bedwig!" he called as he ran. "It's Peace Pax Friends!"

But there was no Mr Bedwig to be found. Not in the cloakroon or the washrooms or the rattling empty classrooms. Simon searched them all. The basement light was still shining but Mr Bedwig was not there either.

"He must have gone home," said Simon at last, trudging back through the echoing school when a sudden movement caught his eye. It was in his own classroom and it was Mr Bang Bang Jones.

"Ruining them!" he heard Mr Jones exclaim, stooping over a table laden with collages of autumn leaves. "Ruining them! Gluing leaves on bits of paper! And dancing in the playground! Dancing! It will have to be stopped!"

Suddenly, like a sort of warning, Madeline's words came back to Simon.

'It would be terrible if Old Bang Bang got rid of Miss Gilhoolie.'

"I shall need them back for research in the very near future and they will be absolutely ruined!"

At that moment a quiet voice behind Simon remarked, "I should go home Young Percy! It is more than time," and Simon spun round and there was Mr Bedwig.

"Peace Pax Friends, isn't it?" asked Mr Bedwig. "And very nice too."

"Oh …!" began Simon.

"Kingdoms have been signed away for less! Now off you go home."

Simon wanted to ask, "Who told you it was Peace Pax Friends?" He wanted to say, "Look at Mr Jones! Wouldn't it be awful if Mr Jones got rid of Miss Gilhoolie?" And he would like

to have asked more about the sweet shop
agency, and the Percys from the past, and
conditions in the ark, and Mr Bedwig's
opinions on hot-air ballooning holidays, and
the possibilities of birthday wishes ever
coming true.

But he said, "Yes Mr Bedwig."

And went home.


On his way down Pudding Bag Lane Simon
stopped to have a look at the sweet shop. It
was closed as usual. He could not remember
ever having seen it any other way.

"It opens when absolutely necessary," said
Gran, when he mentioned it that night.

"Is that where you got Guinevere from?"

"Yes indeed," agreed Gran brightly. "I
ordered her at the beginning of summer as a
matter of fact. I told them what a dreadful
time you were having at school and they

suggested that she would be just the thing."

Guinevere, who had been perched on the curtain rail listening to this conversation, flew down to the tea table and landed beside

Simon's plate.

"Just the thing," repeated Gran with satisfaction. "Dear Guinevere!"

"I wish I could take her to school on Monday," said Simon. "Then Miss Gilhoolie would see her properly. Do you think I could? Her cage could stand on the Interest Table. There's nothing on it yet."

"Nothing of interest?"

"Nothing at all."

"Then you must certainly take Guinevere," said Gran.

On Monday morning there was a surprise waiting for Class 4b. The classroom walls, previously a hideous and scabby peppermint green, were painted sunshine yellow. The ceiling was sky blue. Patches of broken plaster on walls and ceiling had been transformed into an assortment of green and red dragons.

"Mr Bedwig!" exclaimed Miss Gilhoolie.

"You are a genius!"

"It is a knack I picked up from my old dad," said Mr Bedwig. "There was nothing he couldn't do with a paintbrush and a pot of bright red."

"It is absolutely wonderful," said Miss Gilhoolie, who was dressed in bright red herself that morning, very short and shimmering and with diamonds in her hair. "Superb! Goodness Simon! Whatever have you there?"

"It's Guinevere," said Simon shyly. "For the Interest Table."

"She is the perfect finishing touch," said Miss Gilhoolie. "But now to work! Mathematics, Class 4b! Volume and Capacity! It is on the National Curriculum so we must try and take it seriously ..."

This sounded quite worrying but Class 4b soon discovered that Volume and Capacity,

with real sand and water to measure, was
nothing like any Maths lesson taught by
Mr Bang Bang Jones. They were completely
engrossed when the door flew open and the
headmaster erupted into the room.

"WHAT is going on in this class?" roared
Mr Bang Bang Jones. "What? What! Kindly
explain Young Miss!"

"It is Volume and Capacity, dear Mr Jones,"
said Miss Gilhoolie soothingly.

"Volume and Capacity!" roared Mr Jones,
staring at the piles of sand. "It is Buckets and
Spades!"

"Well, naturally ..."

"There are shells in the sand and goldfish in
the water!"

"To add interest and discourage spillage,"
explained Miss Gilhoolie.

"And I must say that I consider you most
unfittingly dressed ..."

"Oh Mr Jones," protested Miss Gilhoolie, smiling. "All Paris knows that diamonds go with anything!"

"AND WHAT HAS HAPPENED TO THESE CLASSROOM WALLS?"

"I came by a drop of emulsion," said Mr Bedwig, appearing from nowhere.

"Outrageous!" spluttered Mr Bang Bang Jones. "They must instantly be repainted Educational Green!"

"That cannot be," said Mr Bedwig calmly. "That cannot be as I have used up the last of the Decorating Allocation for the next twenty years."

Mr Bang Bang Jones glared at Mr Bedwig, purple with temper, and then all of a sudden his eye was caught by a movement on the Interest Table.

## CHAPTER FOUR

"Simon dear, do not roar like that!" begged
Miss Gilhoolie. "Mr Bedwig and I cannot think
when you howl! Guinevere is only confiscated,
remember! She is not gone for good! Oh dear!
Somebody find his diary for him please! It will
give him something to occupy his mind. Good
girl Madeline! And he'll need a pen."

"I've given him a pencil," said Madeline.
"Because of the tears."

*Mr Jones has confiscated Guinevere,* wrote Simon.

"You had better not do any more until the paper gets less damp," said Madeline, and she took his diary away and draped it over a radiator to dry. It took quite a long while, and during that time Miss Gilhoolie and Mr Bedwig tried without success to recover Guinevere.

Miss Gilhoolie went first. She left the door propped open behind her so that she could keep an eye on Simon's tears. This meant that Class 4b, sitting as still as mice, could hear all that went on in the corridor outside the headmaster's door.

"Mr Jones," called Miss Gilhoolie, having knocked and received no answer. "It is I, Miss Gilhoolie. I must explain that I am entirely to blame. It was I who encouraged the children to bring their treasures to the Interest Table. Do let me come in and apologise."

"Too late Miss!" snapped Old Bang Bang.

"Class 4b are very important research material! I will not have them distracted by parrots!"

After that Mr Bedwig had a go, clumping up to call through the keyhole that there was a burst water main in the playing field that the headmaster really ought to inspect.

"I am a professional not a plumber!" shouted Mr Jones through the locked office door.

Then Miss Gilhoolie tried again, saying she had changed her mind about buying the headmaster's lovely books, and asking if she could come in and arrange to purchase half a dozen of all three volumes.

"I have taken note of your order and will have the money taken from your salary," replied Old Bang Bang immediately. "You may go."

"Well," said Miss Gilhoolie, "I suppose it will have to be the diamonds," and she pushed them under the door in an envelope labelled:

She was very cross when old Bang Bang said they were nothing but fakes and pushed them back.

Dougal McDougal suggested that Mr Bedwig turn up the heating so high that Old Bang Bang would be cooked into giving in, but Madeline Brown said straight away, "Guinevere would be cooked too."

So that was not tried, and Mr Bedwig would not let anyone set off the fire alarm either.

"Let me see if he would care for some lunch," said Miss Gilhoolie.

She closed the door behind her and was gone for some time, but eventually returned looking quite pink and indignant and said, "No good Simon, the wretched creature has brought sandwiches! I am afraid you will have to wait until four o'clock. I cannot try again.

He simply won't listen to reason."

There followed a long and anxious afternoon, but towards the end Mr Bedwig cheered them up tremendously by coming in to announce that Guinevere was perfectly safe and well.

"How do you know?" asked Simon.

"Seen her," said Mr Bedwig. "Quite by chance as I was up a ladder cleaning the study windows. Which, by the way, were flung open with great recklessness just as I reached the top pane of glass and I shan't forget that in a hurry. No telling where I would be if I hadn't happened to land on a passing very strong cat! I am going out now for a tin of best salmon. Do not look like that Simon Percy. It is nothing compared to the troubles they had during the Flood."

At four o'clock Simon Percy was allowed into the office to collect poor Guinevere, but

before he could take her away he had to listen
to a lot of rude remarks about who might be
the original Pudding Bag of Pudding Bag
School. And as he listened something in him
stirred, and Simon Percy, descendant of
heroes, found the courage to attack.

"You ought to say sorry to Mr Bedwig!"
he said.

"WHAT DID YOU SAY?"

"I said you ought to say sorry to Mr
Bedwig," repeated Simon. "You bumped him
off his ladder and he might have been hurt
very badly if it wasn't for a passing very strong
cat. And ..."

"YES?"

"You'd better have been kind to Guinevere!"

There was a long silence, during which time
Mr Jones changed colour from white to red
and Simon stood expecting the end of
the world.

"GO!" roared Mr Jones at last.

So Simon seized Guinevere and ran out of the door and he did not stop running until he was out of school and halfway down Pudding Bag Lane. There Dougal McDougal and Madeline Brown caught up with him at last.

"Tell us what happened," begged Dougal McDougal.

"Tell us first if Guinevere's all right," said Madeline.

"She's quite all right," said Simon, displaying Guinevere in her cage. "Did Mr Jones chase after me?"

"No. Was he very cross?"

"He was when I cheeked him."

"You cheeked him?" repeated Dougal.

"Tell us from the beginning," urged Madeline Brown.

"I went in," said Simon, "and he was writing ..."

"More books?"

"No. In a big black file. With a label on the front ..."

"What did it say?" demanded Dougal, hungry for every detail.

"I couldn't read it properly. He covered it up almost straight away. EVIDENCE FOR THE DISMISS something, it began. And then he told me a lot of stuff about Hard Work and Science and then he started on about me being the original Pudding Bag ... don't laugh!"

"We never do laugh!" said Madeline indignantly.

"Sorry. And then I got a very strange feeling, like when you are ill and can't think properly, I told him he should say sorry to Mr Bedwig. And a bit later on I told him he'd better have been kind to Guinevere and then I came away."

"You did exactly what I would have done," said Dougal McDougal in the tone of one who can give no higher praise.

"Evidence for the dismiss?" said Madeline thoughtfully. "Evidence for the dismiss? I don't like the sound of that very much. I don't like the sound of it at all! I hope Miss Gilhoolie's going to be all right."

But Simon was crooning to Guinevere, and Dougal was listing all the other things that somebody ought to say to Mr Bang Bang Jones and nobody took any notice of Madeline.

## CHAPTER FIVE

That night Simon dreamed of school again.
In his dreams Mr Jones was talking.

"Original Pudding Bag," said the dream
Mr Jones. "Dratted parrot! I have brought
sandwiches, sandwiches, thank you Miss! And
I do not like what is happening to Class 4b!
They will be changed beyond recognition and
useless for my research! Impertinent Young
Miss! She will have to go!"

"No, no!" protested Simon, in his dreams.

"Eighteen volumes, she had ordered," mused
the dream Mr Jones (not seeming to notice

what Simon had just noticed, that the dream Simon Percy was clothed entirely in paper, pages from his diary). "Eighteen volumes! Enormous profits! But nevertheless she will have to go!"

Oh, where is my school uniform? dreamed Simon in despair, and not daring to move in case the paper clothes disintegrated around him. Where is it? He will notice in a minute!

But the dream Mr Jones had other things on his mind.

"I shall put it to the Governors that a mistake has been made. She should never have been appointed. I shall present the evidence for the dismiss—"

With a jump Simon was suddenly awake.

"—al of Guinevere Gilhoolie," said the dream Mr Jones.

Simon lay staring into the dark, certain he had not dreamed that voice, straining his ears for the slightest whisper, dreading to hear it.

No sound came.

Gradually his heart stopped pounding so loudly and, at last, he began to drift back into sleep.

"Dratted parrot!" hissed Mr Jones, right into Simon's ear.

"She is ruining that class! They will be useless for research! My work must be considered. The eagerly awaited sequel to PRACTICAL PUNISHMENTS ..."

Simon was wide awake. By means of a small miracle, he was managing not to faint.

" ... SILENCE AT ALL COSTS

THE ULTIMATE GUIDE TO THE CONTROL OF ALIEN LIFE FORMS

Author: Sir B. B. Jones."

I am completely awake, thought Simon wildly.

"Sandwiches," continued Mr Jones. "I have

brought sandwiches thank you Miss! Simon
Percy, the original P—"

All at once Simon could bear it no longer.
He threw back the quilt, turned on the light
and plumped indignantly up in his bed.

"I don't like being called ..." he began
furiously.

"—udding Bag," said Guinevere.

The relief and astonishment was like a
sudden burst of stars.

"Dratted parrot!" said Guinevere again,
in exactly Old Bang Bang's voice and Simon
found himself laughing. He could not help it.
He was so glad to find himself safe in bed,
safe in pyjamas, and to know that it had been
Guinevere all along.

Brilliant, wonderful Guinevere! thought
Simon. Without doubt she must be the most
intelligent cockatoo in the world!

"Look at that radiator!" continued

Guinevere, completely unaware of the shock she had given her owner. "Bangs and blue flashes! That idiotic caretaker has wired it to the mains!"

Simon chuckled happily.

"I must collect evidence! Evidence, evidence! Evidence for the dismissal of Guinevere Gilhoolie."

There won't be any to collect, thought Simon. Miss Gilhoolie is perfect!

*From the diary of Simon Percy. Tuesday, 12th September*

*You won't believe what happened yesterday, I said to Dougal and Madeline this morning as we walked to school, and I told them about Guinevere in the night. I thought they would just laugh. But they didn't.*

*'To recapitulate,' said Madeline Brown, who is very clever. 'Guinevere has overheard Old Bang Bang's secret plan. He does not like Miss Gilhoolie. He thinks she is*

spoiling us and he is collecting evidence so that he can make the Governors get rid of her. And then he will take Class 4b back again. And he will use us to research his horrible new book which is called SILENCE AT ALL COSTS. It sounds ten million times worse than PRACTICAL PUNISHMENTS. This is very serious.'

'It is Old Bang Bang who should be got rid of,' said Dougal. 'I wish he had stayed in Outer Space. It's a pity he ever came back. Simon Percy, do you have to write everything down in that diary of yours?'

Yes I do.


For as long as he could remember Simon had had a feeling that he was missing something. He had never quite been able to keep up with the world around him. He had never quite grasped why he was there. With the arrival of his diary he suddenly understood. He was the one who wrote it all down.

Madeline and Dougal watched as Simon leaned against the playground railings and wrote his last few words. As they stood there a crowd began to collect close by. At the centre of the crowd was Samantha Freebody, also a member of Class 4b.

"What's the matter?" asked Madeline, seeing Samantha's anxious face.

"It's a letter of complaint from my mum," said Samantha, passing a sheet of blue writing paper to Madeline. "Read it!"

*Dear Miss Gilhoolie,* read Madeline,
*It was wrong of you to teach the children to dance the Highland Fling. Our Samantha did it upstairs and it has cracked the kitchen ceiling. Also she has been over excited since the start of term and now she is asking for diamonds. Kindly do not put ideas in our Samantha's head.*

"Fancy having to give poor Miss Gilhoolie that when she's been so kind!" said Samantha, sniffing. "Lending me her diamond necklace when I fell over and cut both knees and making the dinner ladies stop giving me gravy ..."

"You mustn't give that letter to Miss Gilhoolie!" interrupted Madeline decisively. "Notes from home get put in the register and that means Old Bang Bang will see it. It is exactly the kind of evidence he wants to get rid of Miss Gilhoolie. You must get rid of it! Not in the bin, it might be found."

"How then?"

"Eat it!" said Dougal. "That's what you must do. It shouldn't take long! It is only short!"

Samantha saw immediately that he was right, and she hurried to do as she was told. She just managed to gulp down the final fragments as Miss Gilhoolie appeared among them.

"Such a lovely windy day," said Miss Gilhoolie cheerfully. "I thought we would devote the morning to kite-making ... Mr Bedwig has popped out to the sweet shop to collect what we shall need ..."

The bell rang as at least a dozen people tried to tell her how hopeless it was to ever try to buy anything from the Pudding Bag Lane sweet shop.

"Line up! Line up and stop worrying!" said Miss Gilhoolie, "It opens when absolutely necessary."

Sure enough, it was not long before Mr Bedwig arrived, laden, at the classroom door. He had bought coloured paper, balls of string, glue, bamboo and a large bag of pearly fresh mushrooms which he explained were for his lunch.

"Lovely mushrooms! Fresh as fresh," he remarked placidly. "I shall do them in butter

with a sprinkle of nutmeg."

"We will have to have a mushrooming expedition of our own one day," remarked Miss Gilhoolie. "Write it down in your diary Simon and remind me next week!"

Not even the arrival of Miss Gilhoolie's books spoilt that happy morning.


*They came by lorry in three big boxes*, recorded Simon in his diary.

*'Push them under the Interest Table,' said Miss Gilhoolie, 'and we will try and forget about them.' But when Mr Jones came in to snoop he noticed them straight away.*

*'I trust they are not my books,' he said.*

*'Yes indeed,' said Miss Gilhoolie. 'They will be safe under there. Completely undisturbed.'*

*Mr Jones marched out of the room then but he came back almost straight away and said 'KITE-MAKING' in a very cross voice.*

'Quite right,' said Miss Gilhoolie.

The kites worked beautifully.

"Art, design and technology, observation of weather conditions, exercise, fresh air and local space exploration," said Miss Gilhoolie in reply to Mr Jones' rude comments about time wasting.

"There will be complaints from parents if this sort of thing goes on!" snapped Mr Jones, and Samanatha, overhearing, swallowed.

*Madeline called a class meeting after school last night,* wrote Simon in his diary the next day. *So now everyone knows what Guinevere heard while she was being confiscated. And everyone is going to be very careful and show notes from parents to Madeline before they hand them in.*

'You can always tell Miss Gilhoolie what the notes were about if you are feeling guilty,' said Madeline. 'It is the written evidence that is dangerous.'

Miss Gilhoolie says if we do Maths all morning then this afternoon we can go conkering in the park.

'Old Bang Bang won't think much of conkering,' said Dougal McDougal.

'Then we will call it a scientific expedition' said Miss Gilhoolie, 'and do not call him that again, please Dougal.'

'He'll want to come,' said Dougal.

'Well, then we will just sneak off,' said Miss Gilhoolie getting a bit cross with Dougal. 'I cannot be worrying about what will upset Mr Jones all the time. There is a trapdoor that Mr Bedwig has very kindly made under my desk leading straight to the basement and a tunnel out to Pudding Bag Lane from there where the coal used to come in. We will get out that way and he will never know we are gone.'

'Awful if he finds out,' said Dougal.

'Dougal McDougal do you want to go out through the basement tunnel (which I hear Mr Bedwig has lit with old Christmas tree lights) and go conkering in the park, or not?' asked Miss Gilhoolie, so Dougal shut up and we are going straight after lunch. Miss Gilhoolie says she knows a brilliant tree. And she says we can take the kites for when we have got enough conkers and on the way there we are going to stop at my house for Guinevere and Gran.

School never used to be like this, wrote Simon.

## CHAPTER SIX

"Is that homework, Simon?" asked Gran one evening.

"It's my diary," said Simon.

Simon's diary was now quite famous in Pudding Bag School. As well as all the news of that term it had become almost a biography in places. At different times special friends had been allowed to look. Both Miss Gilhoolie and Mr Bedwig had read of the loss of Simon's parents when he was six weeks old.

Simon's account of the hot-air ballooning holiday in the foothills of the Himalayas, and the postcard that had arrived three years later, caused Miss Gilhoolie to mop her eyes and sniff.

"Show Mr Bedwig, Simon dear," she said at last. "Perhaps he will be able to think of something."

Mr Bedwig read in silence for several minutes and then cleared his throat and said, "Well."

"Well what?"

"I shall have to have a think."

"Have you got an idea then?" asked Simon eagerly.

"I can't say I have just at the moment. Ten years is a long time, Young Percy."

"I know," said Simon. "I know it is."

"I could ask around. Get some advice."

"It doesn't matter."

Mr Bedwig began to say something, stopped, and changed the subject.

"I am planning a proper wopper of a bonfire on that spot where the mobile classroom was last year," he told Simon cheerfully. "There is enough rubbish in this school to build a dozen. What do you say to having a real old fashioned Bonfire Night and you can light the touch paper?"

"Thank you very much," said Simon.

"That's a good lad," said Mr Bedwig. "I know nothing about the Himalayas but perhaps it is just that they are finding it a long way back."

"Your trapdoor under Miss Gilhoolie's desk has been very useful," said Simon, sorry to see Mr Bedwig looking so downcast.

"Has it now?"

"We've been conkering," said Simon. "Roller skating, apple picking and we went to the cinema with the apple-picking money, and today we're going on a mushroom hunt."

"And why not?" said Mr Bedwig. "You are

only young once. You mind what you pick this afternoon though. No toadstools! You don't want any more letters of complaint to dispose of."

Simon completely agreed. Letters of complaint were becoming rather a problem.

"We cannot be careless," said Madeline. "Mr Jones is getting worse than ever. He searches for evidence all the time. Simon and I have watched him after school from Simon's bedroom window, going through the bins. If your parents must write letters try and make them do it on rice paper. You can buy it at the bakers and it is easier to chew."

The mushroom hunt led to a major problem in evidence disposal.

*Monday, 24th September*
*Everyone in Class 4b has stomach aches and it is*

Dougal McDougal's fault. It is because of the toadstool he found on the mushroom hunt.

'Do not pick that toadstool Dougal,' Miss Gilhoolie told him. 'It is not the sort of thing we want on the Interest Table. It is Highly Dangerous. There is enough poison in that to put you to sleep for a fortnight.'

She made Dougal put it down and he did. But then he had a thought, and that was that a fortnight is fourteen days. And he remembered that he had seven sisters. So that toadstool, he worked out, would be just the right size to give him two days peace from each of them.

He secretly took it home and squeezed out the juice.

Then he made seven cups of toadstool juice coffee, one for each of his sisters.

Dougal's sisters are a big nuisance to him, but when they had drunk the coffee he suddenly got worried and he told his mum what he had done. His mum said he was a very naughty boy and now his sisters would have to be stomach pumped.

*This happened.*

*Afterwards Dougal's mum wrote a very long letter of complaint to Miss Gilhoolie. Fifty-three pages.*

*'Class effort,' said Madeline Brown when she saw it. 'Two pages each and the extra one for Dougal.'*

*That is why we all have stomach aches.*

*A lot of people are saying we cannot go on like this.*

## CHAPTER SEVEN

Madeline, Dougal and Simon held a crisis
meeting in Simon's bedroom, a room so small
that the only way they could all fit in was by
sitting in a line on the bed. Opposite them, on
the table under the window, was Guinevere.
She had been given a bowl of sunflower seeds
and was picking through them delicately while
listening to the conversation. Every now and
then she looked at Madeline and blinked
one eye.

Oh Guinevere! thought Madeline, poor
Guinevere! I think that perhaps you are going

to have to be very brave.

Out loud Madeline said, "It is turning into a battle between Mr Jones or Miss Gilhoolie. One of them will have to go and I hope it won't be Miss Gilhoolie. I just wish I knew how Old Bang Bang was getting on with his evidence."

Simon knew what was coming then, even before Dougal said the actual words.

"Guinevere could find out," said Dougal.

"Only if Simon really doesn't mind," said Madeline.

"He didn't hurt her last time, did he?," Simon said bravely. "Or frighten her?"

Guinevere shook her feathers and looked scornfully down her beak at the suggestion that she might be frightened of such an earth-bound creature as Mr Bang Bang Jones.

"So you'll take her in again?" asked Dougal.

Simon nodded.

"We'll all do it together," said Madeline, and
Simon was slightly comforted.

The next morning Guinevere, her cage newly cleaned and loaded with provisions, was carefully carried across the playground by Simon while Madeline and Dougal walked solemnly behind.

Mr Bedwig was the first to see them.

"Simon Percy," he exclaimed. "I would have credited you with more sense!"

"It is for a very good cause," Simon told him.

"And what might that be?" asked Mr Bedwig. "It is Trouble Making and Pushing Your Luck if you ask me. Now hop it before I get cross!"

But already it was too late to hop it. Mr Jones was bearing down on them at full speed, and moments later Guinevere had been thoroughly and completely confiscated for the second time that term.

Even Miss Gilhoolie found it difficult to be

sorry for Simon that morning.

"After all the trouble we had last time," she exclaimed. "I warn you I shall not be offering my diamonds again!"

"There is more to it than meets the eye if you ask me," said Mr Bedwig, who was in and out of Class 4b all that morning, busy assembling a slide to go under the trapdoor. "Now then, Miss Gilhoolie, I shall need a volunteer to test this contraption in a minute."

"It is very good of you to take so much trouble," said Miss Gilhoolie.

"No trouble at all," replied Mr Bedwig. "I thought of a fireman's pole, but it wouldn't have done for a lady. Right, I'm ready. Choose me a victim and we will see how it goes!"

Miss Gilhoolie said she thought the whole class should have a go, while she guarded the door. This was done, with much happy laughter and talk of the bad old days when Mr

Jones had treated them as alien life forms. Word had spread that Madeline Brown was going to think of something that would prevent those awful times ever returning.

"Why me?" wondered Madeline, and then reflected, "I suppose there is only me." At the back of her mind was the idea that there was something she could do, a solution to their problems, if only she could discover it. It glimmered in her mind like a distant star on a misty night, nearly invisible.

But definitely somewhere, thought Madeline.

Guinevere was released at four o'clock and Mr Jones made no secret of the fact that she had spent the day under a pile of old curtains.

"She might have suffocated!" squeaked Simon indignantly and Mr Jones said he should have thought of that before he brought her to school.

That night she began talking the moment
Simon switched off the light. Madeline had
told Simon that birds learnt better in the dark.
It must have been very dark indeed under
those curtains, thought Simon, listening in
admiration.

"There is no Evidence!" growled Guinevere
furiously. "Evidence, evidence. Silence at all
costs! Class 4b are being utterly ruined!
Utterly ruined! Lost to me, lost to me and
I have no research!"

It was beginning to sound quite sad,
thought Simon.

"No research," lamented Guinevere. "No
evidence. No appreciation of my methods.
Science is the only thing that matters in the
end. I should like to see the lot of them
blasted into Space!"

He always ends up with space, thought

Simon. He is obsessed.

But Guinevere had not finished yet.

"They are research material, I told her, and you treat them like pets! Horrid little children! If I only had the money I would leave this world tomorrow! I should go back to my old life! Back to ... back to ..."

Guinevere's voice fell gradually silent.

She's had a very long day, thought Simon, and watched lovingly as she tucked her head under her wing, and fell asleep.

"Back to his old life?" asked Madeline when Simon saw her the following Monday. "Are you sure that's what he said?"

"Yes," said Simon. "He's been saying it all weekend. I mean Guinevere has. And talking about his great work."

"SILENCE AT ALL COSTS," said Madeline, nodding wisely.

"Yes that one," agreed Simon. "And he says

we are horrid little children only any use for research. And that is all except for stuff about evidence again."

Madeline looked very thoughtful and later she went across the playing field and inspected Mr Bedwig's bonfire site.

*Diary of Simon Percy. Thursday, 2nd October*

*Dougal McDougal has been off school all this week. I always used to think he was lucky because he only has to sneeze and his mum and his sisters put him to bed with comics and hot lemon and telly in his bedroom.*

*But poor old Dougal being ill this week. There has been a "Headteachers' Conference" in London so Old Bang Bang hasn't been in school for three whole days.*

*On the first day our class had a chestnut roast in the basement and on the second we did a play for Mr Bedwig. It was called The Thirty-Ninth Day and everyone dressed up as animals. We used the fire hoses* for rain outside, and our classroom was the ark.

Mr Bedwig said it was as good as the real thing and he should know.

Today we had tests all morning which Miss Gilhoolie marked at lunchtime.

'You are all far in advance of most children your age,' she told us. 'Which just goes to show what a good teacher I am because you certainly weren't a few weeks ago. I shall reward myself by going to the circus and you can come too. It is supposed to be an excellent one. Real flying horses, they told me at the sweet shop, and no poor tame lions ...'

'At the sweet shop?' everyone asked.

'Where I got the tickets,' said Miss Gilhoolie.

I didn't think there would really be flying horses but they were definitely horses and they did fly. We all had goes on them afterwards. Over a safety net in case we fell off. But nobody did.

So poor old Dougal, missing all that.

Simon and Madeline went to visit Dougal after
school that day. They found him sitting up in
bed and very eager to hear the latest news.

"Has anything important happened?" he
demanded at once.

"Not since we got Guinevere confiscated
again and you know about that," said
Madeline.

Simon pointed out that there had been the
Noah's Ark play (with fire extinguishers), the
circus and the chestnut roast, and Madeline
said Oh Yes, but those things were not really
very important.

"Exciting isn't always important," Madeline
explained.

"What circus?" demanded Dougal, bouncing
about in bed. "What chestnut roast? What
Noah's Ark play?"

"Never mind all that now," said Madeline.
"There's something I've been thinking about

that matters much more. Listen for a minute."

But Dougal did not want to listen for even a second and he turned his questions upon Simon.

"I'm no good at talking about things," said Simon. "You'd better read my diary."

So Dougal began reading Simon's account of all that he had missed, first to himself, and then aloud.

And after that he read backwards though the entries until they ended up at the very first morning of term.

There followed a long silence.

"A lot has happened," said Dougal at last. "I'd forgotten half of it. It's a jolly good diary, Simon. What's the matter, Madeline?"

Madeline had been staring at Simon as though stunned, but Dougal's question seemed to wake her up again. She took the diary from him and weighed it in her hands.

"It's much too big," she said eventually.
"Even for a class effort. We should be really
ill."

"What do you mean?" demanded Simon.

"Perhaps Mr Bedwig could put it in the
boiler. I can't think how else we could get rid
of it."

"GET RID OF IT?"

"Simon," said Madeline. "There is enough
evidence in this diary for Mr Jones to get rid
of Miss Gilhoolie tomorrow! It doesn't miss
out a single thing! Mr Bedwig's slide and the
secret tunnel and all the evidence we've eaten
and everything we did while he was away. And
loads of other things too. All Mr Jones would
have to do is show it to the Governors and
that would be that. It is highly, highly
dangerous. Letters of complaint are nothing
in comparison."

Then Simon Percy and Madeline Brown

had an enormous argument.

"I'm not getting rid of it," said Simon, and Dougal McDougal backed him up.

Then Madeline flounced off in a huff and Simon, out of gratitude to Dougal, allowed him to borrow his diary for the night so that he could read again the amazing account of all that he had missed.

Dougal solemnly promised not to let it out of his sight until Simon collected it the next day.

The next day two important things happened at once.

The first was that Miss Gilhoolie started them off on a Scientific Art project.

"We will draw space rockets," said Miss Gilhoolie, "and we will stick them all around the walls. They will go nicely with the dragons and I hope very much that they will also cheer up Mr Jones."

The second important thing was that Dougal McDougal came back to school.

"You did bring my diary, didn't you?" asked Simon, the moment he saw him. "You didn't leave it behind?"

" 'Course not." Dougal dumped his over-flowing school bag on to the cloakroom floor with a sigh of relief. "Hang on a minute and I'll find it."

Simon looked doubtfully at Dougal's school bag and thought it would take more than a minute. He was already feeling slightly alarmed, but Dougal obviously had no worries at all.

He began unpacking.

Out came Dougal's PE kit and one muddy trainer. Two comics with the backs pulled off. A large packed lunch. A burst open packet of crisps.

"Hurry up," said Simon anxiously.

"Coming, coming," said Dougal airily.

A pencil case with a broken zip. An empty coca cola tin. A broken calculator. A plastic bag full of very old conkers. Several handfuls of notes and letters to and from school (never delivered).

"It's not there!"

"It is! Somewhere." Dougal dragged out two woolly hats, a Pudding Bag School sweatshirt (Aged 6–8 years), and part of an Action Man.

"That's stuff you've had in your bag for ages!"

"Bother!" said Dougal. "But I did put your diary in! I know I did!" and he turned the whole bag upside down and shook a litter of sweet wrappers, odd socks, and lego on to the cloakroom floor.

"You've lost it," said Simon in horror.

"Or left it at home. Might you have left it

at home?"

"No. I know I didn't. I put it in and then I remembered my packed lunch ..."

At that moment Mr Bedwig came in with his arms full of lost property.

"Dougal McDougal," he exclaimed when he saw the heap on the floor. "I have never seen the like! This is a Place of Education not the Council Tip! Get that lot picked up before you say another word! I might have known it was you! You've left a trail clear back to the gates."

Then they saw that the Lost Property he was carrying all belonged to Dougal. His other trainer. His reading books. Two comic covers, a handful of crisps, a broken ruler and a note addressed to Miss Gilhoolie explaining why he had been away.

"But where is my diary?" wailed Simon, scuffling frantically through the piles of rubbish on the floor. "Didn't you find my diary

Mr Bedwig?"

"I can't say I did," said Mr Bedwig.

Madeline was so cross with Dougal that she could hardly bring herself to speak to him, but she managed, despite the awful quarrel of the night before, to be quite nice to Simon.

"Try not to worry too much," she whispered, pale with worry herself. "Mr Jones may not have found it. And I have had an idea to rescue us and save Miss Gilhoolie at last. I am sure it will work. I have asked Miss Gilhoolie if she minds if I do a model of a

space rocket instead of a picture and she says
I can."

Most of Madeline's message meant no sense
at all to Simon. Nor had he much hope that
Mr Jones had not found his diary, and he
could tell from Madeline's face that neither
had she. By lunchtime they knew that the
worst had happened. A series of enormous
notices appeared all over the school.

They all said exactly the same thing.


EXTRAORDINARY AND URGENT
GOVERNORS' MEETING TO BE HELD

SUBJECT: SUDDEN ALARMING EVIDENCE
FOR IMMEDIATE DISMISSAL OF CERTAIN
MEMBER OF STAFF.


"And why are you looking so down in the
dumps, young Simon?" asked Mr Bedwig,

seeing Simon studying one of these notices.

"Mr Jones has found my diary," moaned Simon. "The one that me and Dougal were looking for this morning. I lent it to Dougal and he lost it. That is the sudden alarming evidence those notices are about. It is just what Madeline Brown said would happen last night."

"That young lady has more sense than all the rest of you put together if you ask me," remarked Mr Bedwig. "She knows What's What. We have had many a chat and I cannot fault her on theoretical parachute jumping so I have no doubt she is right about this too. I will see what can be done."

To Simon's immense relief his diary was restored to him before the start of afternoon school.

"I happened upon it," said Mr Bedwig,

"while attending the locks on the headmaster's private safe. I have had a quick glance. Circuses and toadstool picking and escape tunnels and I don't know what! Whatever made you write it all down?"

"I had to," said Simon.

Mr Bedwig shook his head, but all he said was, "Well, you take it home and leave it there. Sudden and alarming evidence is what it is, and no mistake. I may not be able to rescue it so quick another time."

The notices vanished as rapidly as they had appeared once Simon had his diary back. But now Mr Jones knows it exists, thought Simon. It was an uncomfortable thought.

"I cannot bear the way he looks at me," he told Madeline.

"Perhaps you won't have to much longer," said Madeline. "I shall be able to tell you my idea soon, I think. But first, would you mind if

I borrowed some of your books? *Junk Modelling that Works, Anybody can do Anything, Metal Work for Beginners* and that new one you've just got."

"They're very boring," said Simon.

"No, they're not," said Madeline. "You'll see."

The day after that Madeline borrowed *How Does it Go?* and *A Child's Guide to Modern Technology.* In Scientific Art she appeared to do nothing but read, occasionally slipping down Mr Bedwig's slide to consult him in the basement.

"Madeline dear," said Miss Gilhoolie, "are you sure you're not working too hard?"

"Quite sure," said Madeline. "I am only getting on with my model. I will tell you when it's finished Miss Gilhoolie."

"Thank you," said Miss Gilhoolie.

## CHAPTER EIGHT

Miss Gilhoolie was staring at Madeline's work for Scientific Art. It was a piece of paper about the size of a tablecloth with several smaller sheets attached behind. It looked like a pattern of cobwebs, dozens of cobwebs, layered on top of each other. Hundreds of red pencil arrows led to hundreds of tiny labels. The pages underneath were almost exactly alike, except that the cobweb patterns were different colours and the minute labels were not the same.

"But I thought you were making a model,"

said Miss Gilhoolie at last.

"It's a plan of a model," said Madeline.

Miss Gilhoolie peered at some of the tiny labels.

"Mn.Prb.lv." she read. "Mn.Prb.E. Mn.Prb.Fs." They made no sense at all.

"Well," said Miss Gilhoolie, giving up. "It's very nice Madeline dear, and I can see you have worked very hard ..."

"Mr Bedwig helped a lot," said Madeline modestly. "Would it be all right if you didn't stick it on the wall, Miss Gilhoolie? I should like to take it home, if you don't mind."

Miss Gilhoolie said of course she did not mind and Madeline took her Scientific Art project home and showed it to her father. He peered at it for several hours and at last announced that he saw no reason at all why it should not work.

"But I hope you won't be leaving us quite

yet?" he remarked rather wistfully as he handed it back to Madeline. "I should be very sorry ... er ... sorry ... er ..."

"Madeline," supplied Madeline. "And you need not worry. It is for somebody else, not me."

"Delighted to hear it," said Madeline's father warmly. "Any advice you might need, just ask ... er, Madeline. Always pleased to help with homework, as you know!"

This offer, and her father's statement that he saw no reason why her design should not work, encouraged Madeline very much. So much that she called a class meeting the very next day. It was held in the middle of the playing field so that there could be no possibility of being overheard.

"This is the problem we have got," began Madeline, plunging straight in. "Mr Jones is planning to get rid of Miss Gilhoolie as soon

111

as possible. He thinks she is spoiling us. She treats us like proper human beings instead of alien life forms and that is no good for Mr Jones. He has decided she has got to go and he will be our class teacher again. He wants to use us for his new book which is called SILENCE AT ALL COSTS THE ULTIMATE GUIDE TO THE CONTROL OF ALIEN LIFE FORMS."

There was a murmur of indignation from Class 4b. "He cannot just get rid of her without any excuse," went on Madeline, "so he has been collecting evidence ..."

"But I thought we'd been eating all the evidence," interrupted Samuel. "We have eaten stacks of evidence Madeline, you know we have."

"We have not eaten everything," said Madeline. "We have not eaten Simon's diary. Mr Jones found it earlier this week and if it had not been rescued so quickly that would have been the end of Miss Gilhoolie. I am afraid he will get his evidence one day, I am sure he will. Samantha, crying will not help."

"I can't bear the thought of being an alien life form again," sobbed Samantha. "And I do like Miss Gilhoolie!"

"All of us do," said Madeline, "and that is why I have thought of a plan to solve all our problems ..."

Class 4b sighed with relief.

"I think we should build a rocket," said Madeline, as calmly as one might say, 'I think we should make a cake'. "Mr Jones does not like being a headmaster. He would much rather be an astronaut. If he had a rocket he would be off like a ..."

"Rocket," finished Dougal McDougal. "But this is completely daft! You don't know how to build a rocket Madeline Brown!"

"Yes I do. I worked out a plan in Scientific Art," said Madeline, holding up her bundle of cobweb diagrams as proof. "Simon lent me some books that explain how it should be done, and Mr Bedwig says he will help with the welding, and my father has told me that he can see no reason why it should not work …"

There was a stunned silence.

"I thought we could build it on Mr Bedwig's bonfire site," Madeline went on. "That way we can cover it up with bits of bonfire when we have to come away and leave it. Mr Bedwig has already fixed up some scaffolding made out of odds and ends from the PE cupboard which will be a great help … Yes, Samantha?"

"Does Miss Gilhoolie know?"

"Of course not," sighed Madeline. "She would want to know why, and it would hurt her feelings tremendously to hear how much

Mr Jones wants to get rid of her. Besides, she would start asking questions about other things. All that evidence we have eaten for a start. She would not be pleased about that. Now, this is my idea. When the rocket is finished I shall take Mr Jones to the bonfire site and say, 'Mr Jones, you wanted to go back to your old life and now you can. Here is a rocket …' "

"Rockets," interrupted Dougal McDougal, "need rocket engines! Have you thought of that Madeline Brown?"

"Yes I have," said Madeline, "and you can order them from NASA. They deliver within forty-eight hours. The only trouble is they cost quite a lot and you have to be over eighteen. But Mr Jones has all that money he got for his books from Miss Gilhoolie and he is a lot older than eighteen. And I am sure that when he sees his own private rocket, all finished and provisioned and ready to go except for the engines, he will order them at once and off he will pop and all our troubles will be over. I hope. Any more questions?"

There were no more questions, Madeline's friends being struck dumb with surprise, so Madeline continued.

"It will have to be another class effort, this rocket building, and we will have to do it when Mr Jones is not around. That will mean early mornings mostly, and perhaps a bit in the evening between six and seven when he goes to the chip shop for his tea. Somebody will have to be up on the roof of the school keeping watch down Pudding Bag Lane ..."

"My binoculars!" interrupted Simon excitedly. "We could use my birthday binoculars, Madeline!"

"Brilliant," said Madeline. "Thank you Simon! Also we are going to need scrap iron, heat-resistant paint, rivets, light bulbs, computer parts and nourishing food, so if anybody …"

Madeline's enthusiasm was suddenly catching. At least a dozen hands shot up with offers of donations.

"And we will need a way to keep it secret when we're not working on it," said Madeline. "It is no good Mr Jones seeing it before it is done. He'll just say it's another of Miss Gilhoolie's ideas and get rid of it."

"We can camouflage it!" squeaked Samuel. "I can bring my brother's old army tent."

"It's not going to work," interrupted Dougal suddenly. "All this is just rubbish! Even if you could get enough rocket parts and fix them together it would take years!"

"Not with all of us helping, and Mr Bedwig too," argued Madeline. "You know what a fast worker he is! And he has promised to see what he can come by in the way of bits and pieces and he says there is always the sweet shop if absolutely necessary ..."

The mention of the sweet shop and the promise of Mr Bedwig's help convinced even the most doubtful. Madeline suddenly felt very tired. "That is the end of the meeting," she said thankfully, and sat down to thunderous applause.

From that moment on the secret rocket project became a success. Sheet metal, star maps, paint and provisions were donated in unlimited quantities, begged by Class 4b from their friends and relations.

For security reasons no grown-ups were allowed into the secret, except for, of course, Mr Bedwig, Madeline's father (who now spent many hours checking computer programs in the belief that he was helping with homework), and Simon's gran, whose kitchen window happened to overlook the launch pad.

"I am sure it is safe for my father to know," said Madeline. "Most people never listen to a word he says. Only bonkers professors take any notice of him. And that doesn't matter because nobody takes any notice of them."

"People don't listen to Gran either," agreed Simon. "They just say she is wonderful for her age. Let's invite her to come and look properly! After all, she did buy all the instruction books."

"Let's invite them both," proposed Madeline, and this was agreed.

The rocket was very nearly complete when Simon's gran and Madeline's father paid their visit. The enthusiasm of Class 4b, the tremendous efficiency of Mr Bedwig, and the quite astonishing way in which Pudding Bag

Lane sweet shop supplied endless vital rocket components (while remaining firmly closed to all passing trade) had combined to work wonders.

It was an impressive sight. It rose above Mr Bedwig's enormous bonfire in a five metre high shining tower. At the top a fluted dustbin lid had been shaped and polished into an elegant shining cone. The port holes (old washing machine doors) were also polished. The emergency exit was outlined in gleaming red paint, and the entrance door was edged in holly green. The whole of the rest of the rocket, including the four large dustbins at its base which would one day hold the engines, had been sprayed with Non-Stick-Heat-Resistant-Radiation-Proof-Easy-Clean-Anti-Mildew-Guaranteed-Rust-Retarding-Glitter-Effect-Silver paint. (Supplied, Mr Bedwig told them, by the sweet shop.)

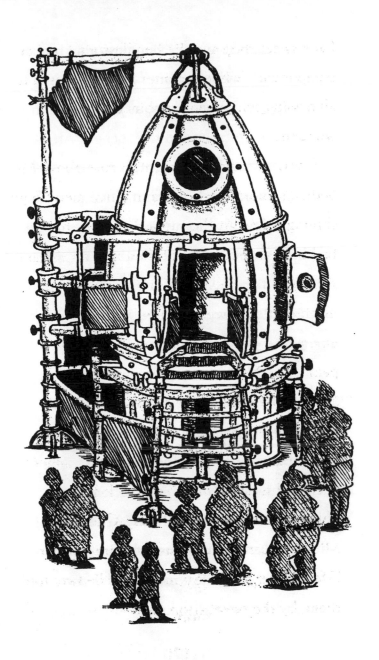

"It is a remarkable achievement for a class of ten-year-olds," said Madeline's father.

"Yes indeed," agreed Gran, as she peered into the crowd that surrounded the rocket. "Ah, there is dear Madeline! I must go and give her this parcel. It is a Keeping Fruit Cake to set him on his way. And also some packets of seeds. Peas, carrots, onions, parsley and potato, just the basis of a good Vegetable Soup ..."

She hobbled away to where Madeline stood in the centre of an admiring crowd.

Dougal McDougal was on look-out duty that morning, high up on the school roof. He felt very left out, alone up there, watching Madeline the centre of so much attention.

"She is getting a bit big-headed these days," he said crossly, as he watched the scene. "It's only a perfectly ordinary rocket! Without engines. It looks exactly like any other rocket.

Probably smaller actually. And it wobbles!"

"It wobbles!" he told Madeline later on when he was back on solid ground again.

"It just needs something heavy in the base. I'm going to use Mr Jones' PRACTICAL PUNISHMENT books. I'll ask to borrow them. Miss Gilhoolie won't mind."

"I suppose you think you're jolly clever," said Dougal, who was tired and cold and grumpy from sitting so long on the roof. "But you'd never have managed without Mr Bedwig, and all the stuff you've had from the sweet shop! All this fuss is just showing off!"

Samantha happened to overhear this, and she rushed to the rescue at once.

"Madeline never shows off!" she told Dougal. "About anything. You're just jealous Dougal McDougal because she thought of it and you never could!"

Dougal became crosser than ever.

"Madeline Brown isn't the only person who can think of things," he growled. "You wait. I'll show you!"

"How?" demanded Samanatha and Madeline.

"Wait and see," said Dougal.


*Dougal and Madeline are quarrelling again,* wrote Simon in his diary that night. *They have not been friends since Dougal lost my diary. I wish he hadn't. Old Bang Bang is always glaring at me. He is looking for my diary, I am sure. He is in and out our classroom every day.*

*'Drat the miserable man!' said Miss Gilhoolie.*

*She has lent Madeline Brown all her boxes of the PRACTICAL PUNISHMENT books.*

*'Would you be cross if they got a bit changed?' asked Madeline.*

*'What sort of changed?' asked Miss Gilhoolie.*

*'Hot,' said Madeline.*

'You can roast them for all I care,' said Miss
Gilhoolie. 'They are Utter Bunk. Good grief! Here is Mr
Jones AGAIN! What can we do for you THIS TIME
Mr Jones.'

'I am just checking the items on your Interest Table,'
said Mr Jones. 'No parrots, I trust.'

'Certainly not,' said Miss Gilhoolie. 'The children
keep their treasures safely at home these days.'

'Keep them at home, do they?' asked Mr Jones.
'Thank you very much Young Miss!'

He stayed away after that.


After that last entry, life in Pudding Bag
School was never quite the same again.

## CHAPTER NINE

"Friday!" Madeline had announced on Monday afternoon. "He could be off by Friday. There's just a little bit of painting to finish. We can do it tomorrow, and on Wednesday I will take Mr Jones to see his rocket. The engines will take no time to fit, it is just a matter of slotting them into the dustbins. If he orders them straight away he should easily have them by Friday!"

"Friday," Dougal McDougal had repeated scornfully. "And today's only Monday! That's no good! That means he's still got a whole

week to collect his evidence. Fat lot of good
it will be launching Old Bang Bang into space
if he's managed to get rid of Miss Gilhoolie
before he goes! You want to get rid of him
a lot sooner than Friday, Madcline Brown."

"I want to," Madeline had agreed. "But I
can't. No one could. And don't say you could,
because you couldn't!"

"Oh couldn't I then?" said Dougal.

It took Dougal a long time to solve the
problem of how to show Madeline Brown that
she was not the only person in the world who
could think of things.

It was very difficult because Madeline had
thought of a rocket.

Which meant that Dougal had to think of
something more spectacular than a rocket.
Dougal left the school playing field and was
wandering down Pudding Bag Lane racking his
brains, but no good ideas seemed to come. At

the sweet shop he stopped to re-read the
poster and to try the door handle. Lately it
had begun to look quite shiny from the
persistent efforts of Class 4b to come in and
buy something absolutely necessary.

So far, however, the sweet shop had remained stubbornly closed. Nor did it open for Dougal, but just as he touched the handle inspiration came to him. Madeline's rocket had one great flaw. It had no engines. It could not be launched into space without the co-operation of NASA and Mr Bang Bang Jones.

Now he had a plan! A joke! A huge surprise for Class 4b and Madeline Brown in particular! Something that would make Madeline exclaim: "I wish I'd had that brilliant idea! I wish I'd thought of doing it like that!"

When Madeline said that, Dougal decided, everything would change. Straight away he would tell her how good her rocket was, and he would apologise to Simon for losing his diary. He would become once again his usual modest, charming and wonderful self.

"But Madeline has to say it first," said Dougal.

Simon Percy closed his diary, pushed it under his pillow and switched off his bedside light. This was Guinevere's signal to begin. She had never forgotten the time she had spent as a prisoner of Mr Bang Bang Jones, and she seemed determined that Simon should never forget it either.

"... Original Pudding Bag!" exclaimed Guinevere. I have brought sandwiches, sandwiches, thank you Miss! ... Evidence, evidence! Evidence for the dismissal of Guinevere Gilhoolie ..."

Her nightly recital was becoming as familiar to him as the chimings of the church clock across the road.

Simon reached under his pillow just to make quite sure that his diary was still there.

"Research material and she treats them like pets ... Silence at all costs!"

"Oh shut up Guinevere!" moaned Simon,

but very quietly because he knew she could not help it.

".... Bangs and blue flashes coming from the radiator! That idiotic caretaker has wired it to the mains!"

Simon always rather liked that bit.

"How I wish I could go back to my old life!"

"Friday," murmured Simon, drowsily.

It was dark black. It was the middle of the night and there was no moon.

"Evidence! Evidence! Evidence!"

Bother Guinevere! thought Simon, fast asleep.

"Silence at all costs!"

Simon groaned and slid down in bed so that the quilt covered his ears.

"Dratted parrot!"

Simon, still dreaming, burrowed completely under the bedclothes.

"Evidence! Evidence! Evidence!" shrieked Guinevere, every feather quivering.

The dark figure that stooped over the bed turned around and glared. Long white fingers groped over the bedside table, under the pillow and grabbed.

The grab woke Simon at last. He sat up and a gust of freezing air hit him in the face. A clattering sound came from the street below. The bedroom window was wide open and the curtains were streaming into the room on the cold night wind. Guinevere was frantic and his diary was gone.

Dougal lay awake that night making plans, and the next morning he set to work.

The first thing he needed was a day off school to arrange everything. This was no problem at all. His mother and father departed early for work leaving his seven adoring sisters

in charge. It only took a little sighing, and a
groan or two to make all seven of them look
at each other and decide poor darling Dougal
had been working too hard.

"Take a day off, Dougal!" they urged as they

whirled around the house in a chaos of
hairdryers, lipsticks and magazines, so
Dougal did.

The next thing he needed was money.
Quite a lot of money. This was also easy.
He borrowed it from his sisters as they dashed
past, late as usual for their buses and tubes
and offices and appointments.

"Take what you like Dougal Darling!" they
said, handing over notes and cash and
handfuls of credit cards while he straddled the
doorway like a highway man. "Take what you
like BUT GET OUT OF THE WAY!"

By lunchtime, only Dougal and his
youngest elder sister, Kate, were left in the
house. Kate was very pretty and very good
natured and easily Dougal's favourite sister.
Also she was over eighteen (which mattered
very much) fond of shopping, and had passed
her driving test.

Kate agreed at once to drive Dougal in the family minibus to Pudding Bag Lane.

"Whereabouts in Pudding Bag Lane?" she asked.

"The sweet shop," said Dougal.

"But it's always closed."

"It opens when absolutely necessary," said Dougal, "and will you do the actual buying please Kate, because it's the sort of shopping where you have to be over eighteen, please please Kate, brilliant Kate, you do look good in that top and those jeans with your hair like that, you are the best sister in the world, I'm so sorry you had to be stomach pumped ..."

"Dougal," interrupted Kate sternly, "why do you have to be over eighteen?"

While Dougal and Kate were shopping, Pudding Bag School was in turmoil. The story of the burglary of Simon's diary had spread like magic.

Nobody had any doubts about who the burglar must be.

"Old Bang Bang," said Simon bitterly.

Very soon notices began to appear.

EXTRAORDINARY AND URGENT
GOVERNORS' MEETING
TO BE HELD TODAY!

OBJECT:
INSTANT DISMISSAL OF DANGEROUS
AND INCAPABLE MEMBER OF STAFF

"It is very sad," said Miss Gilhoolie to Samantha when she found her crying over one of them. "But Mr Jones is quite right. Dangerous and incapable members of staff should be dismissed!"

"But Miss Gilhoolie," sobbed Samantha.

"Don't you know who he means?"

"No," said Miss Gilhoolie, "and to try to guess would not be kind! Now, books away! Spelling Test time! All the words you have learnt this term!"

This was a very dismal prospect because all term Miss Gilhoolie had handed out ten words a night, five nights a week, and it made a very long list. They were about halfway through when the door crashed open.

"Number one hundred and twenty-nine," said Miss Gilhoolie.

"Mephistopheles. Good morning Mr Jones!"

Mr Jones did not reply. Instead he stood and shrieked with laughter. He howled. He rocked with glee, doubled up. He pointed a trembling finger at Miss Gilhoolie and hugged his chest and screeched.

It was a horrible performance.

"He is choking," declared Miss Gilhoolie

suddenly. "Mr Jones, I will pat your back. Madeline dear, please fetch Mr Jones a glass of water ..."

But Mr Jones had gone as suddenly as he had appeared.

"Oh," said Miss Gilhoolie as the door slammed behind him. "Well. Number one hundred and thirty. Philosophy. What has anyone noticed about the last ten words?"

"They are PH words Miss Gilhoolie," said Madeline Brown.

"Quite right Madeline," said Miss Gilhoolie. "Now, on to the dinosaurs! Number one hundred and thirty-one. Diplodocus!"

"Perhaps," said Madeline at lunchtime, "Mr Bedwig will be able to help."

But for once Mr Bedwig was no help at all.

"It's beyond me this time," he said. "I had a

look round his office first thing but it was not there. It is my belief he has it on his person. There is no help for it to my way of thinking."

"Oh Mr Bedwig!" wailed Simon and Madeline.

"Don't you come Oh Mr Bedwigging me!" said Mr Bedwig, poking gloomily through a box of broken table-tennis bats. "Look at this lot! There are not two the same size! What can't be cured must be endured. Now go and put that last drop of paint on that rocket before the bell goes."

"What's the point?" asked Madeline. "Mr Jones will have got rid of poor Miss Gilhoolie long before it's ready to launch. Dougal McDougal was quite right. Everyone is saying so now."

"Be that as it may," said Mr Bedwig. "You must prepare for all eventualities. Noah built that ark through a record-breaking drought

and I've got something here for you, young
Madeline which I hope you will never need. I
happened on it quite by chance," he
continued, handing her a large parcel, and I
thought of you at once."

"What is it?" asked Simon, inquisitively.

"Never you mind," said Mr Bedwig. "It is not
something as wants packing and unpacking
more than is strictly necessary. It is an
Emergency Precaution in case of the
Unexpected. You keep it with you, Madeline.
Better safe than sorry when it comes to
rockets!"

"Thank you very much," said Madeline,
seeming to understand completely.

"Off with you then," said Mr Bedwig, and
handed her the paint.

Meanwhile Dougal and Kate had driven to the
sweet shop and Kate had gone inside, leaving

Dougal to look after the minibus.

"But I want to come in too," Dougal had protested. "Why does it need looking after?"

"Because last time I borrowed it, it got stolen," said Kate. "And two times before it got driven into. And every other time I've locked the keys inside by accident. So say you will Dougal darling, or else I won't do any shopping for you at all!"

"All right," agreed Dougal, although it seemed to him that the hardest part of his whole plan was to be forced to wait outside in the minibus while his sister Kate turned the handle of the Pudding Bag Lane sweet shop and went inside.

She was back out again very quickly.

"What an interesting place!" she said, hopping into the driver's seat, starting the engine, and pulling out without looking in front of a double-decker bus.

"Oy!" cried Dougal. "Watch out Kate! And why are we going? Aren't we going to load them up? Didn't you buy any?"

"Ever such a nice boy serving," said Kate. "They're being delivered."

"What do you mean, delivered? Kate! Those traffic lights are red!"

Kate did a perfect controlled emergency stop, took out a hairbrush and began to tidy her long blonde hair.

"Delivered means they bring them for you," said Kate, fishing a lipstick out of her bag and beginning to apply it very carefully. "You should know that Dougal! Oh, bother these lights! They never give you time to do anything."

"Please tell me what happened in the sweet shop," begged Dougal as Kate swerved into a bus lane and began humming happily to herself.

"Well. I said, 'Hello! Gosh, how absolutely

wonderful to find you here, and he said, 'Tell
me your name and what are you doing on
Saturday? Have you anything planned ...' "

"WHO DID?"

"Peter from the sweet shop, of course! How
many times have I been round this roundabout,
Dougal? I'm getting tired of it! Hang on!"

Dougal clenched his teeth and shut his eyes.

"There we are," said Kate. "Yes well, so then

I asked 'Do you sell fireworks, please?' and Peter said 'Certainly darling, for you I would sell the moon and stars, any particular sort?' So I said 'Rockets'. That's what you wanted isn't it?"

Dougal nodded.

" 'Rockets,' he said. 'How many are you thinking of?' OH DOUGAL! THE POOR LITTLE SQUIRREL! OH, THE POOR LITTLE SQUIRREL! Oh, it's all right. I'm going to stop somewhere. Through that gap."

"It's St James's Park."

"I know. Lovely ducks. 'Four dustbins full my brother needs,' I told Peter. 'For his school project. He goes to Pudding Bag School, poor little soul!' He seemed a bit surprised."

"Oh did he?"

" 'We thought they were doing it through NASA,' he said. 'Ready to go then, are they?' What did he mean, Dougal?"

"Nothing. Go on."

"Well, so I asked which brand of rockets was best and Peter said  The InterGalactic Special Effect Milky Way Wanderers. And I said they sounded perfect."

"They do," agreed Dougal.

" 'Delivered and packed?' asked Peter. 'Packed and delivered you mean!' I said. But Peter said, 'No, delivered and packed. We can put them in the bins for you if you'd like. In fact, I'll get on with it straight away!' He wouldn't let me pay. He said he'd put it on the account. He couldn't have been more lovely!"

Brilliant, wonderful Kate! thought Dougal, and out loud he said, "You did everything perfectly!"

"It was a pleasure," said Kate. "Look Dougal! Four policemen! You hardly ever see four policemen all together! I hope there's nothing wrong with the ducks ..."

Then Kate was arrested.

"Tell Peter!" she screeched over her shoulder as they led her away.

Somehow or another the afternoon at Pudding Bag School dragged past. Half-past three arrived and Class 4b were dismissed with their usual spelling list and the awful feeling that once the Extraordinary and Urgent Governors' meeting had taken place there would be nobody to care whether they knew the words or not.

"We will always love you Miss Gilhoolie," sobbed Samantha as they lined up to go home.

"I should hope so too," said Miss Gilhoolie.

Madeline and Simon did not leave straight away. They hovered in the quiet corners of the playground, waiting for the moment when the Governors would assemble and the Extraordinary and Urgent meeting would begin.

Dusk fell over the playground The school became dark and silent, except for the lighted windows of Mr Jones' office. Madeline and Simon could see him in there, arranging chairs for the fatal meeting. Occasionally he stopped work to double up in silent laughter.

"There's your diary!" said Madeline suddenly, and there it was, battered and unmistakable, on Mr Jones' desk.

"I wonder where he's had it all day."

"He's taking it with him now."

Mr Jones vanished then, but reappeared a few minutes later, silhouetted in the open doorway of the main entrance, rocking on his heels. The Governors were due any minute and victory was within his grasp at last.

In his fists he clutched Simon's diary.

Suddenly Simon started to run. Hurtling out of the shadows, he charged across to Mr

Jones, seized the diary and fled. As he ran he tried to think. Where could he hide?

Home was impossible, there were Gran and Guinevere to be considered. Pudding Bag Lane was dark and uninviting. The playground was an empty waste.

There was a flurry of motion and Madeline was beside him. "Quick Simon, he's just behind!" she had time to pant, and then Mr Jones arrived, thundering round the corner and the chase began.

It was like some awful game of tag. Simon ran and ran, backwards and forwards across the playground, swinging round corners, sprinting across the places where the light streamed out from windows, hugging his diary, dodging and leaping and always with Mr Jones one breath behind.

"Drop it! Drop it!" roared Mr Jones.

A stitch had begun in Simon's side and he

was finding it hard to breathe. It became like a dream and he ran in his sleep. He stopped being frightened and then became terribly frightened, and then tripped.

"Ha!" panted Mr Jones in victory, and the next moment the diary was plucked from Simon's hands.

Not by Mr Jones.

Just in time Madeline had seized it, and she ran with it straight to the place that had filled her thoughts for days. Straight to the bonfire site and Mr Jones' rocket, and Mr Jones ran after her.

It took Dougal a very long time to get from St James's Park to the Pudding Bag Lane sweet shop. It was nearly dark when he arrived. He hurled himself at the door and it opened before he touched it so that he landed on the chest of a large young man.

"Just closing," said the young man, removing Dougal and depositing him in the street. "Not absolutely necessary, is it?"

"Kate said, 'Tell Peter!'" gasped Dougal. "My sister Kate! She's been arrested!"

"Kate who bought the rockets?"

"Yes, yes! In St James's Park!"

"I'll get there at once."

"Are you Peter then? Did you deliver them?"

But it was no good. Peter was already sprinting down Pudding Bag Lane, his hair on end and his jacket flying open, charging to the rescue. As he turned the corner something fell out of his pocket. Dougal followed him and picked it up.

It was a box of matches.

Dougal stood alone in the darkening lane and thought triumphantly, "I've done it!"

No need now to wait for engines from NASA, the rocket was complete and ready to go. He had beaten Madeline Brown.

I'll just go and have a look, thought Dougal.


Madeline reached the rocket with no clear plan in mind except perhaps to lock herself in with Simon's diary and stay there, if necessary, until morning. That would stop the Governors' meeting going ahead at least, and during the night she might think of something better. It was not a very good plan but it was the best she could do.

She reached the rocket, and then things began to go wrong. The darkness was confusing and she was out of breath. The handle of the door was harder to turn than she had anticipated. Mr Jones' footsteps had been muffled on the grass, but suddenly his puffing was very close. He was much nearer than she had expected.

Before she could shut the door he had

sprung forward, seized the handle, and climbed aboard after her.

Dougal McDougal heard nothing of the chase. He came up to the bonfire site just in time to see Mr Jones clamber aboard the rocket before the door slammed shut.

Then Dougal had a stupendous and terrible idea.

There was Mr Jones' rocket, finished at last. There was Mr Jones inside it. The bonfire was ready and the engines were in place, four dustbins full of InterGalactic Special Effect Milky Way Wanderers.

There was a box of matches in Dougal's pocket.

The temptation was too great.

Dougal sprinted across the shadowy, trampled grass, pulled out the matches, and lit the bonfire.

"That'll surprise Madeline!" he thought, and he pictured her arrival in the morning to find the bonfire burnt and the rocket gone and all their troubles blasted into space. "By me!" thought Dougal, happily.

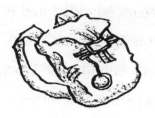

## CHAPTER TEN

The flames took hold almost at once and
Dougal prudently retreated to the middle of
the playing field to watch from a safe distance.
There he was astonished to find Simon Percy,
wheezing terribly, and staggering towards him.

"Dougal! Dougal! Quick!" croaked Simon
flapping his arms in a kind of slow motion of
despair. "Quick Dougal! We've got to call the
fire brigade! Someone's lit the bonfire!"

"I know," said Dougal smugly. "It was me."

Simon goggled at him.

"It's a surprise for Madeline."

Simon could make no sense of this.

"The fire brigade," he repeated frantically. "You go. I can't run anymore."

"Don't be daft, Simon!" said Dougal. "You don't want to miss the best bit do you? It's going to take off any minute."

"Take off?"

"Those dustbin engines are stuffed full of firework rockets! InterGalactic Special Effect Milky Way Wanderers!"

Even as Dougal spoke there came from the bonfire site a most enormous fizzing pop.

The ground rocked beneath their feet.

The entire end of the playing field became a glowing cloud of greenish purple smoke.

A terrible hissing roar began to fill the night. It grew louder and louder and constellations of stars began hurtling from the bonfire. Simon's legs gave way completely. He collapsed on to the grass and shut his eyes.

It felt like he was witnessing the end of the world.

Beside him Dougal said, "There she goes!"

Simon's eyes opened to an unbelievable sight. Madeline's rocket rising straight up to the sky in a cloud of stars. Rainbow and silver coloured stars that leapt in curves from the dustbin engines and vanished with pops and whistles and coloured smoke.

"Guess who's on board?" said Dougal complacently, gazing up as it climbed.

"Madeline," moaned Simon.

"No! Twit! Old Bang Bang Jones!"

"And Madeline."

"Don't be daft."

"She is. I saw her. She was saving my diary. Mr Jones was after her ..."

"Mr Jones," said Dougal, "is on the rocket! I saw him! He climbed on board and the door banged shut ..."

"He climbed in after Madeline."

"NO!"

"YES! HE CLIMBED IN AFTER MADELINE."

"HE DIDN'T."

"HE DID. HE CLIMBED IN AFTER MADELINE. MADELINE'S IN THE ROCKET."

"I WON'T LISTEN. I'M NOT LISTENING."

"SHE'S IN THE ROCKET. SHE'S UP THERE NOW."

"Say you're joking," begged Dougal.

"I'm not joking. Look at me. I'm not joking."

Dougal looked at Simon's desperate face and saw that it was true. He wasn't joking.

They stared at each other for one horrified moment, and then their eyes turned back up to the sky.

There was nearly nothing to be seen.

A small blur of light. A smudge of cloud that seemed to sparkle. That was all.

Inside the rocket it was very bumpy. Bumpy and dark, pitch black, with blinding white flashes.

At first Madeline and Old Bang Bang were too startled to do anything but hold on, but after a while the motion became smoother, Madeline found the light switch, and they were able to dodge the quite astonishing amount of loose objects that were tumbling about them.

But neither of them said a word. Old Bang Bang's mouth was hanging open and his eyes were bulging out of his head but he did not make a single sound. Madeline thought it was like being at a terrible party where no one can bring themselves to break the quiet. She heard her voice say, "I can't think why it took off."

Old Bang Bang's answer seemed to come from far, far away. "What took off?"

"This. This rocket we made for you."

"Rocket."

"Yes. For you. Because you said you wanted to go back to your old life."

"You made this?"

"Yes."

There was an even longer silence, broken only by the sound of external explosions. Madeline began to feel terribly awkward.

"It's very small," said Old Bang Bang.

"It will look better tidied up," said Madeline. "It's only meant for one person really."

"One person? One person?"

"Yes," admitted Madeline, as she stacked and tidied. "Well, just you really, you know ..."

"You are telling me that this rocket was designed to carry one person alone?" interrupted Mr Jones.

"Yes. I really shouldn't be here."

"No you shouldn't," shouted Old Bang Bang Jones, suddenly leaping into action. "You certainly shouldn't! Think of the weight. You are extra weight!"

"Perhaps we should throw out the ballast."

"The ballast?"

"PRACTICAL PUNISHMENTS. You know, your books? We were using them for ballast because Dougal said it wobbled, but we won't need them anymore, will we? We could thr—"

"Throw out PRACTICAL PUNISHMENTS," roared Old Bang Bang, "With new worlds to conquer? You silly, silly child! Out you get!"

"What?"

"Out! Out!" repeated Old Bang Bang. "What are you waiting for? I must be on my way!"

"But Mr Jones ..."

"I hope I have made myself perfectly clear?"

"Yes, yes," said Madeline, "but, Mr Jones, you don't know how to fly it ..."

"Mere common sense!"

"Or where things are. There are star maps, and a first aid box and Simon Percy's gran's fruit cake which she said ought to be kept wrapped up for another two weeks ..."

"I cannot listen to all this chatter! Out you go! You are wasting my time!"

"I will, I will," said Madeline, desperately. "It will be quite all right. I have an Emergency Precaution. You need not worry ..."

"I am not worrying," said Old Bang Bang coldly, as he fumbled with the lock on the Emergency Exit. "Ah! There! Got it! Off you go!"

He would have thrown me out anyway! thought Madeline suddenly. Emergency Precaution or not! Dear Mr Bedwig. Oh, Dearest Mr Bedwig! And I always knew

Theoretical Parachute Jumping would come in handy.

A blast of cold air suddenly filled the rocket.

"Now then," said Old Bang Bang, hustling her toward the icy black hole. "Out with you! Before I get cross!"

"Yes," said Madeline bravely, "But Mr Jones ..."

"What is it now? I need to shut the door!"

"Only, there are sandwiches under the black box that need eating straight away. And a hot water bottle ..."

Mr Jones gave a hard push and Madeline suddenly found herself swinging by her finger tips from the edge of the hole.

"Let go at once!" snapped Mr Jones.

"Are you quite sure you wouldn't like to come too?"

"Let go at once!" shouted Mr Jones, so Madeline let go.

Madeline never forgot the few minutes that
followed, free falling through the solar system,
fumbling with frozen fingers to undo the
straps of her school bag.

"The view was amazing," she said. "The
stars all around and the moon right by my
feet, and all the lights of London spread out
below. I know I should have enjoyed it."

"Didn't you then?"

"Only in a way."

Simon and Dougal also never forgot those minutes. Quite a crowd had gathered at the bonfire site. Miss Gilhoolie and Mr Bedwig, who had been visiting the sweet shop and had rushed back to school at the sound of the first explosion. Guinevere and Gran, and Madeline's father who had popped in on them for tea. All the School Governors. Every passing stranger. They all, every single one of them, knew what Dougal had done.

Dougal had told them.

There was a breathless hush on the field that night. Nobody could do anything but stare at the patch of night sky where the rocket had last been visible.

For a long time they saw nothing.

Then a tiny speck of movement appeared in the blackness, travelling so fast that it was only a blur of motion.

"It's a bit of rocket," said Simon.

"It's Madeline," said Miss Gilhoolie, and there was absolute silence.

She fell like a star, plummeting, and then, at the moment when the crowd on the ground could bear to look no longer, something changed, and she fell like an autumn leaf.

"Good girl," said Mr Bedwig approvingly. "She's found the rip cord!"

An enormous parachute, gold as an autumn beech tree, now billowed above Madeline's head.

"I came by that," said Mr Bedwig, wiping a tear from his eye, "not two days ago. I gave it to her just in case."

"I think she's still got my diary," whispered Simon.

"She's waving," said Dougal, "and listen! What is she shouting?"

"I can't think why it took off!" shouted Madeline.

## CHAPTER ELEVEN

Dougal, Madeline and Simon met outside the sweet shop before school the following morning. The window was empty. The door was wide open. A notice was propped on the counter.

*SIMPLY THE BEST SUPPLIES AND SERVICES!*
(it said in curly letters)

*For Household Pets, Professional Staff,*
*Vacuum Cleaner Parts.*
*Dry Cleaning, Spring Cleaning, Caretakers and Cooks.*
*Fine Jewels, Fireworks, First Class Free Advice.*

*Enquire Within!*
*All Needs Supplied!*
*Everything Guaranteed Best In All The World!*

Underneath, in ordinary writing, someone had added:

Due to the early completion of work in this area we have moved to a new location.

"They've gone then," said Simon, and stood and wondered and wondered, until Dougal and Madeline, said, "Come on, we'll be late."

"There's something very odd about that sweet shop," said Dougal as they walked slowly on to school.

"Not any more," said Madeline sadly.

*From the diary of Simon Percy,*
*Pudding Bag School,*
*Pudding Bag Lane,*

*London,*

*England,*

*Great Britain,*

*The World,*

*Space.*

*Monday, 20th October*

*Miss Gilhoolie came to school today in silver leather*

169

jeans and all her diamonds.

'What do you think, Simon?' she said and I said, 'Oh Miss LeatherGilhoolie, Oh Miss LeatherGilhoolie you do look lovely and shiny.'

'That's right Simon,' she said. 'It may not be National Curriculum but it is very important to remember that anything goes with diamonds.'

Dougal McDougal is being very kind to everyone. When Madeline heard about why her rocket took off she said, 'Firework rockets! Oh Dougal! I wish I'd had that brilliant idea! I wish I'd thought of doing it like that!

Madeline is feeling a bit guilty because she didn't bring Old Bang Bang with her when she parachuted down. She did ask him, but she didn't like to try and persuade him, she said, in case the parachute didn't open. Because up until then she had only done theoretical parachute jumping and she wasn't sure she could do it in real life. But Miss Gilhoolie said, 'Do not worry Madeline. I am sure he is much happier where he is.'

*Kate has fallen in love. (But at least she did not go to prison).*

*Now that Mr Jones has gone Mr Bedwig is Acting Head of Pudding Bag School, but he is still caretaker too.*

*'It has happened before,' he says, 'even Old Noah wasn't above getting down with a bucket when the need arose. But that was a Short Term Arrangement due to an Emergency.'*

*'So is this,' said Miss Gilhoolie, 'and I expect you will get double pay while you do it.'*

*'Money,' said Mr Bedwig. 'I do this job for love not money! And Short Term it may be, but I am not finished yet.'*

*He is still sorting out the table-tennis bats.*

*'I need a nice big red,' he said, 'and a nice big green. And then I will be done.'*

*I bring in Guinevere every day now, to keep Mr Bedwig company when he is having to be Headmaster. She has*

learned to say a lot of things that are much nicer to
listen to in the night, and she has learnt to whistle a song
that Mr Bedwig sings to her.

> Oh Guinevere, Sweet Guinevere,
> The years may come, and the years may go,
> But still my heart holds memories dear
> The dreams and songs of long ago.

And I think it's lovely.

And so everything is all right. Nearly all right. But I
never got my birthday wish and now that the sweet shop
is just a sweet shop again I don't suppose I ever shall. I
am exactly ten years and six weeks old now.

I wished it had been years, not days. Then they
would have been back quite soon.

That was my birthday wish. Never tell, Gran said,
but writing is not the same as telling.

I wish it had been years, not days.

For a few moments Simon stared at the words he had written and in his mind he was back once more at the end of summer in the park on the last day of the holidays. He saw again the short dry grass of the birthday picnic, the hot shimmer of the candles and the leaf that had landed like a star on his cake, exactly the colour of Miss Gilhoolie's hair. Madeline, happening to glance at him, knew at once that his thoughts were far, far away from Class 4b, Pudding Bag School.

"Miss Gilhoolie," said Samantha. "Look outside. Look at Mr Bedwig with those table-tennis bats! Why is one red and one green?"

"He's waving to something," said Samuel Moon.

"CRIKEY!" shouted Dougal McDougal. "CRIKEY! LOOK!"

"Dougal McDougal!" said Miss Gilhoolie, "Sit down and stop shouting! Everyone, sit down and stop shouting!"

But nobody did. Instead, they rushed to the windows, shouting, and Miss Gilhoolie rushed too, and then she said in a very odd voice, not shouting, "Simon, come here!"

So Simon looked dreamily up from his diary to see what all the fuss was about.

And out in the playing field an enormous, ancient hot-air balloon was just touching down.

**More Pudding Bag School adventures:**

HILARY McKAY

**PUDDING BAG SCHOOL**

Cold Enough for Snow

97S 0 840 9701S S

HILARY McKAY

**PUDDING BAG SCHOOL**

A Strong Smell of Magic

97S 0 340 97030 0

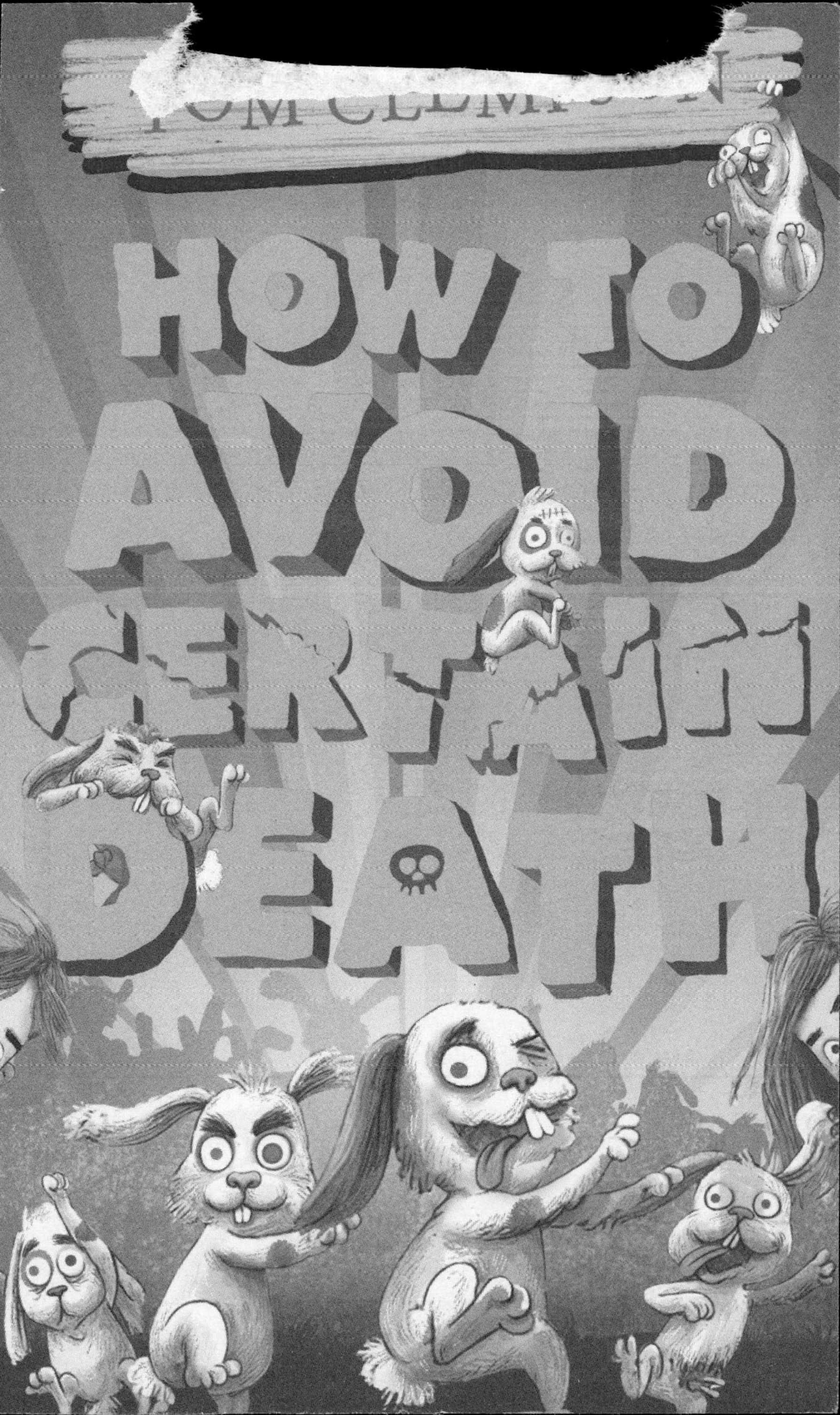
HOW TO
AVOID
CERTAIN
DEATH